# Lightning
# Rider

To Hayley –
I hope you
enjoy this book.
It was a lot of
fun to write!

*[signature]*

# Lightning Rider

Jacqueline Guest

James Lorimer & Company Ltd., Publishers
Toronto, 2000

© 2000 Jacqueline Guest

First publication in the United States, 2001

James Lorimer & Company Ltd. acknowledges the support of the Ontario Arts Council for our publishing
program. We acknowledge the support of the Govern-
ment of Canada through the Book Publishing Industry
Development Program (BPIDP) for our publishing activities. We acknowledge the support of the Canada
Council for the Arts for our publishing program.

Cover illustration: Jeff Domm

**Canadian Cataloguing in Publication Data**

Guest, Jacqueline
    Lightning rider

ISBN 1-55028-721-4 (bound)   ISBN 1-55028-720-6 (pbk.)

I. Title.

PS8563.U365L53 2000      jC813'.54      C00-931895-X
PZ7.G83Li 2000

| James Lorimer & Company | Distributed in the |
| Ltd., Publishers | United States by: |
| 35 Britain Street | Orca Book Publishers |
| Toronto, Ontario | P.O. Box 468 |
| M5A  1R7 | Custer, WA  USA |
| | 98240–0468 |

Printed and bound in Canada.

*For Diane Young and Ward McBurney.*
*Thank you both for the years of late nights,*
*rushed deadlines and most of all, faith.*

# Chapter 1

January Fournier looked up from her order pad as the wooden screen door to the restaurant banged shut. She was going to have to remind Robin, the owner, to fix that. It was the height of the July tourist season, and tourists didn't like doors that slammed noisily as they entered. Or worse, seemed to chase them out when they left.

A flash of annoyance passed through her as Collin Watson sauntered through the door. He had an attitude that really tried her patience — *I'm here. I'm great. What more could the world want?* His entourage of fawning teenagers of both sexes followed dutifully behind.

Jan sighed, grabbed a handful of menus and headed over to their table. The noise level in the small restaurant had just gone up with Collin's louder voice working on drowning the others out.

"Hey, January, baby." Collin grinned as he took the menu from her. "I bet you were just waiting for me to come in and make your day." He flashed her a $5000.00 orthodontic smile.

"Yeah, Collin, you make working here for a summer job something really special. If it weren't for the whole finish high school, go to university, have a future thing,

I would just stay here and wait for you to drop in. Now what can I get you?"

Collin's face darkened. "Just bring us a couple of extra-large Bragg Special's and a round of orange pop. You think you can handle that?"

Jan smiled sweetly. "I'll try." She was just heading back to the kitchen when the restaurant door banged shut again. She glanced over and saw a tall, good-looking dark-haired man in a Bragg Creek Police uniform heading to the back of the restaurant. She smiled at him and nodded.

It was David McKenna, her favourite constable. They'd been friends ever since David had helped her brother, Grey, when he'd gotten into trouble for shoplifting a few years ago. Even after everything was settled, David had continued to stay close to Grey and her, making sure they knew he was available to talk anytime.

Jan's dad had died in a car crash when she was small, so talking to someone like David was comforting at times, especially since her brother didn't always want to open up to her about so-called guy stuff, such as hairstyles (short or long), clothes (trendy or not), music (grunge or mainstream), oh, and she almost forgot — the finer points of most makes of cars. Her brother was the best anywhere, but sometimes, he had some funny ideas.

David stood beside his usual table, motioning for her to come over. This table was the one used by staff when things got slow enough so that the servers, and usually the cook too, could sit and have a bite to eat or a quick coffee before the next customers came in.

David always sat here so he could visit with the staff as he ate his meal. It was a friendly arrangement and the staff enjoyed his sense of humour and the casual way he could fit into their conversations. He was well liked by

2

all the kids in the community, who made up the bulk of the part-time employees at local stores and restaurants.

Jan smiled at him and nodded, signalling she'd be there in a minute. She thought David looked tired. His face was strained and his bright blue eyes were now sunken and flat-looking. His mouth, which was usually in a perennial smile, was set in a hard line.

"Excuse me, miss, but could we have some more water for our tea?" an elderly man asked as she passed his table on her way to the kitchen with Collin's order. Speaking with the man and his wife earlier, Jan had noticed their accents. It was a game she played as she dealt with the many tourists who came to Bragg Creek. Figure out where the visitors came from without having to ask. She decided these two were from Newfoundland from the delightful way they rolled their words around.

"Certainly, I'll be right back," she said, smiling at the casually clad pair. They both had bright yellow sweat-shirts on with the slogan *I'm spending my kids' inheritance!* emblazoned across the front.

She stopped at the waitress station on her way to the kitchen and grabbed the pot of freshly brewed coffee and a mug. Diverting to the staff table, she set the mug down and poured the coffee in one smooth movement. "Do you need a menu, David, or should I just get you the special?" she asked brightly, hoping her cheeriness would help lift his mood.

He remained standing, his expression serious. Jan immediately knew something was wrong.

"Jan, I need to talk to you, right away," was all he said.

"Sure, just let me take this order to the kitchen." Her throat suddenly felt tight.

She hurried through the gaily painted swinging doors to the kitchen. "Order in!" she called as she quickly wrote the time on the order and stuck the top sheet of the bill in the ticket wicket where Josh Blakeman, the cook, could pick it up.

At seventeen, Josh was a year older than Jan was and, despite his usual reserved attitude, they got along pretty well. Other staff didn't like the way he always kept to himself, never joining in the quick banter that flew between them. They thought he was stuck-up, but Jan liked the way he didn't chatter on about nothing, or worse, gossip about people they both knew. She found if she kept to herself and did her job, working with him was no problem. In fact, she liked his quiet style.

Josh had just come in to start his shift. She watched him as he hung up his old leather coat. He looked like a poster boy for the Four-H club, with his short brown hair and clear hazel eyes framed by perpetually wind-chafed rosy cheeks. He was tall and lanky and by the way his shoulders filled out his cowboy T-shirt, obviously used to hard, physical labour. Jan had to admit, that in his well-faded jeans and cowboy T-shirt, admonishing you to *Quit crying down my back, yer rustin' my spurs*, he looked amazingly good.

He finished tying his apron, then walked to the ticket wicket, took the order and went to the pizza prep area where he would create the famous house speciality.

Jan cleared her throat. "Look, Josh, David McKenna's here and wants to talk to me. He's being really serious and it's freaking me out. I'll take the drinks out to Collin's table and then I'm going to sit and talk to him for a minute. If you need me, I'll be at the staff table."

At the mention of Collin's name, Josh's mouth twisted. They used to be buddies, but lately their friendship had cooled to the point where neither of them spoke. Collin, from a very well-to-do professional family, was spoilt and rich and liked to flaunt it, especially around someone of Josh's hard-working ranching background who he considered beneath ûim. Josh had no time for Collin's airs or superior attitude. They were complete opposites.

Pouring the drink order, Jan headed back out into the dining room.

She set the drinks down at Collin's table, where everyone was laughing and joking and just being generally noisy. At the staff table a grim-faced David McKenna was still waiting.

David motioned for her to sit. As he sat opposite her, she noticed he hadn't touched his coffee.

"What's up, Officer? Was I over the speed limit with that last order?" she asked, trying to force a smile.

"Jan, I have some bad news," he started without preamble.

Her heart began beating rapidly. She was aware of the sudden pounding in her ears. "Is it my mom?" she asked quietly, trying to control the mounting panic.

He looked at her and shook his head. "No, your mom's okay. It's your brother, Grey. He's been in a motorcycle accident — a serious accident while riding in Kananaskis Country."

*K-Country?* Jan thought of the huge forest reserve just a few kilometres west of Bragg Creek. It was a vast tract of land, which was part of the extensive park system that ran through the Alberta Rockies. A haven for campers, it was always busy with hikers, four-wheelers, snowmobilers or cross-country skiers.

But what was Grey doing riding in the reserve at this time of day? She, too, loved to ride her motorcycle in the mountain park and he always waited until she could go with him. Glancing at her reflection in the mirror, she thought she looked strange. Her dark skin and deep brown eyes looked suddenly sallow and sunken. She absently pushed a stray strand of her glossy black hair away from her thin face. This couldn't be happening, not to her only brother.

Jan tried to swallow, but her mouth was dry. "Is he dead?" she asked in a whisper.

"No, but he's been taken by air ambulance to the Foothills Hospital in Calgary. He's in the ICU on life support. It's pretty bad, Jan. I think you should come with me and I'll take you into the city to see him. Your mom's already at the hospital. We had the Calgary police contact her at work. I don't think she should be alone right now." His voice was low and Jan could hardly hear him because the pounding in her ears had just become a lot louder.

Jan thought of her mom being called at work. She was a marketing sales rep for a large insurance broker in the city and being called about an accident your own son had been in must have been a shock. Kind of like what Jan felt now.

"Yeah, sure ..." she said hesitantly. "Ah, just let me call someone to cover my shift." She was having trouble focusing. *He's on life support. It's pretty bad.* Those were the phrases they used when they didn't want to tell you your only brother was going to die.

She went back into the kitchen to phone Robin. Briefly, she told her what was happening. As she said the words, it still didn't seem possible. This was a nightmare. Her brain went into automatic.

Robin's usually cheerful voice was sympathetic. "Don't wait for me to come down, Jan. Just lock the door and put the 'Back in five minutes' sign up. I'll be there in a tick."

In a small tourist town like Bragg Creek, you could do things like that. All the local shops, whose staff was usually one person, used the magic sign. It covered just about any amount of time from a couple of minutes while you ran over to the coffee shop to pick up the lunch you'd ordered, to going over to the local farmers' market on Sunday morning for fresh tomatoes and a quick gab with the ladies who ran the booths. It was a time-honoured system, which no one complained about.

She hung up the phone. "Josh, there's been an accident. Grey's been hurt and is at the Foothills. I've got to go. You can put up the 'five minutes' sign until Robin comes down." She heard herself saying the words. Her voice sounded distant, as though someone else were speaking.

"Sure, Jan. Is he going to be okay?" Josh asked, looking up from the carrots he was dicing for tomorrow's soup.

"I hope so. I'll know more when I talk to the doctors."

She was trying not to think of Grey lying in the hospital. She knew if she did, she'd start crying, and she wanted to stay in control, at least until after she'd seen her mom. She grabbed her jacket and left with David.

It felt odd sitting in the front seat of David's car. She'd never been in a police cruiser before. Some part of her brain absently wondered how long the forty-kilometre drive to Calgary would take in a police car.

"Jan, there's something else you should know," David said as he turned onto the highway.

Jan looked at him, refocusing. "About the accident?" she asked, wondering what next.

"Yes. Grey wasn't on his own motorcycle when the accident occurred. He was on a brand-new Bimota. Did any of his friends have a bike like that?" David's tone was all cop now.

"A new Bimota? Are you kidding? We don't know anyone who could afford a rocket like that." She shook her head. "I have no idea whose bike he borrowed.

7

Didn't the owner call the station when Grey failed to come back with his very expensive machine? "

"That's the part of the puzzle that really bothers me, Jan. The bike was stolen." The constable flicked on his signal light and neatly pulled the big Crown Victoria out and around a slow moving semitrailer, tucking it back into the right hand lane just before the dotted line turned solid.

"Stolen!" Jan said, shocked. She didn't like the implication. "Grey didn't steal any bike, David, let's be real clear on that right from the beginning." She looked over at the police officer, but his eyes remained on the road.

"Okay, take it easy," David said quickly. "I'm not saying he stole the bike. But if he didn't, do you have any idea how Grey would have gotten his hands on it or any other strange bike and what he may have been doing in K-Country with it?" He accelerated the big car just a little.

"I told you, I have no idea. The Kananaskis has always been a favourite place for us to ride. Grey said it relaxed him." Jan suddenly knew where this was going. "You think this is connected to the other bike thefts that have happened here recently, don't you? And that would link Grey to them too." She shook her head. "I don't know why he was on that Bimota, but one thing I'm absolutely sure of — Grey didn't steal that bike or any bike!"

She settled back in her seat, watching the ripening fields of wheat and barley speed by. Outside the window, everything looked so green and pastoral. The wind sent waves rolling through the grain like a gently undulating emerald ocean.

Jan knew she was going to have to get to the bottom of this bike theft. If she didn't, her brother would go to jail for sure. She wasn't going to let that happen, not to Grey.

* * *

The Foothills Hospital was a huge modern facility that hummed with constant activity. It sat on the brow of a hill that overlooked the Bow River valley; The distant western horizon was marked by the jagged outline of the Rocky Mountains. Their peaks still snow-clad, glistening in the afternoon sun.

David walked with Jan as she hurried into the main admitting area. She was directed to a wide hallway with the sign 'Intensive Care Unit' mounted above two closed doors. David pushed a large, round, stainless steel button below the sign and both doors swung open to admit them.

They headed directly to the unit desk. "Excuse me, my name is January Fournier and my brother, Grey Fournier, was brought in earlier today ..." She looked expectantly at the small woman behind the desk.

The ward clerk nodded her head and touched a computer screen with a pen, which was attached by a black cord. "He's in bed three. The doctors are still with him. Perhaps you want to wait with your mother in the family room? It's right down the hall on your right." She smiled and pointed back the way they'd come.

They started down the hallway. As they approached, Jan could see her mother sitting on the couch just inside the door to the brightly lit room. Her face was haggard and drawn and her eyes looked as though she'd been crying.

Jan noticed her mother's fingers noiselessly moving from bead to bead on the old rosary she always carried in her purse.

A touch of guilt washed over Jan as she watched her mother silently praying. Jan hadn't been to Mass for a long time. They used to argue about it, then her mom had said she would light a candle for her and the arguing had stopped. It had been a couple of years ago, right around the time Grey had gotten into serious trouble with the law.

Grey and Collin Watson had been caught stealing a stereo when they were fifteen. They'd decided to go to the Youth Justice Committee instead of regular court.

The Youth Justice Committee was an alternative measures program used by many communities in Alberta. It allowed young offenders to make voluntary restitution for their crime rather than appearing before juvenile court. When they'd completed the punishment meted out by the committee, they would have no criminal record and a second chance to go on with their lives.

The YJC's tribunal was made up of local citizens who volunteered their time to participate in the process. They decided what punishment would be accorded the guilty parties.

Jan remembered going with her mother and Grey to the formal meeting with the YJC. Not only were the members of the committee there, but also the owners of the store. Grey hadn't known Collin was going to steal the stereo, but he'd faced the tribunal along with his friend. He was no rat. Besides, who'd have believed a story about his not knowing Collin was going to steal? He'd told the committee he was sorry for what he'd done and was willing to make restitution.

Jan knew Grey was telling the truth when he'd told her he wasn't in on the stealing, but he was with Collin when it had happened. The owner had seen the two boys in the store and called the police. They'd been caught as they left together.

Jan and Grey both knew things wouldn't have worked out so badly if it hadn't been for the arresting officer, Sergeant Gellar. Of all the police on the Bragg Creek Force, only Gellar had a "thing" for Indian people. The Fournier's were Métis, a mix of white and first nations, but all Gellar saw was the Indian half.

He never came right out and said it, at least not publicly, but any Native who'd ever run afoul of him knew exactly how he felt. When Gellar went out drinking with his buddies and began voicing his opinions, it was obvious he had no use for Indians.

In the cold hard light of day, Sergeant Gellar would never admit to those same opinions. He was always careful to stay within the law and be politically correct in public. He also made sure everyone knew he did — especially important people who could help him in his career.

Jan suspected Sergeant Gellar had used persuasion with one of the members of the Youth Justice Committee to make sure Grey got the stiffest sentence they could mete out. Collin had received what amounted to a slap on the wrist.

Still, it would have been a lot worse if Constable David McKenna hadn't spoken up for Grey. Gellar had originally wanted Grey funnelled into the juvenile court system, where he would have ended up in jail, but David had tipped the balance and Grey's case had remained with the YJC.

Sergeant Gellar had never let Grey forget about the robbery and in a community this small, it was hard to avoid running into people — especially if one of them was a cop. Grey had responded in the worst way possible. He became a problem kid, always looking for a fight, eventually dropping out of school and running away from home.

11

That had been two years ago, and it had left Grey very bitter. Jan had persuaded him to come back home, but he'd refused to go to school. However, thanks to a good word from David McKenna to the owner, Grey had been able to secure a job at the local garage, where he developed his avid interest in motorcycles. In fact, when Jan had bought her '86 Yamaha RZ-350 last winter, Grey had given her a motorcycle road-racing course as a birthday present. He'd said it was so she'd be able to keep up with him. Jan had loved it.

The course had taught her lots of valuable pointers including apexes and cornering, braking, setting the bike on the suspension and even crashing. She needed these, as Grey liked nothing better than to spend hours tweaking up her bike until it was outperforming much bigger machines. Jan thought he was at his best when he was teaching her about synching carburetors or trick-gearing or some other bike detail he considered important.

The list of upgrades he'd done on her bike was impressive. He'd practically rebuilt it. Along with lots of other details, it now sported racy suspension and had been lightened considerably. Porting the heads and oversize pistons had really helped the top end. The last thing Grey had done to her bike was to replace the brake lines with steel-braided ones and get her a solo seat. They'd laughed about what was left to do to her little bike, and apart from blueprinting the engine, Grey was satisfied he'd done everything a brother could do. Her bike was a real rocket.

Jan thought about how her mother had always had to handle everything alone and how tough it had been. Jan had wished for a dad just so her mom would have someone to help her. Now Grey was fighting for his life in a hospital room and, on top of that, faced with the charge of stealing a high-dollar bike. This was going to be impossibly hard for everyone. Jan took a deep breath.

"Hi, Mom," she said, going into the waiting room and giving her mother a big hug. "What did the doctors say? Do they know if he's going to be okay?"

Her mother looked at Jan with worried eyes. "They're with him now. They've been working on him for such a long time." Her face clouded. "I called the restaurant and Ms. Pearce said you'd already left. How did you know about the accident?"

It was then she spotted Constable McKenna waiting in the hall. "Oh," she said, nodding in David's direction. "You should ask the constable to come and sit. I think it will be a while."

Jan smiled at the term *the constable*. Her mom could never be accused of being too informal. Even now she made Jan and Grey call other family acquaintances *uncle* or *auntie*, even though they weren't related at all.

Jan hoped David's presence would help. After all, he was a family friend. Ever since Grey's trouble, David had maintained a personal interest in the Fournier children and Jan knew he and her mom had gone out for coffee several times. In fact, now that she thought about it, David had been there in the wings for a long time now.

The waiting seemed to go on and on. Jan kept glancing at the clock. She was sure the hands were moving in slow motion. Even the second hand was conspiring by halting between numbers as it jerked its way around and around the dial. What was keeping them? Why didn't they come and stop this terrible not knowing? She stood and nervously began pacing the waiting room.

Still restless, she went back to her seat. "Look, Constable," she began. She referred to David by his proper title to appease her mom. "If you have to get back to Bragg Creek for work or something, it's all right. Mom has her car here." Jan looked at David.

"I'm off duty ..." he began, glancing at his watch, "now. And I really don't have to rush back. I was thinking of going and getting something for us to eat — burgers and fries from the cafe here in the hospital maybe. What can I get you ladies?"

Before either of them could answer, a small, balding man in a white coat appeared at the door.

"Mrs. Fournier, I'm Doctor Singh. I'd like to talk to you and your family about Grey ..."

David cleared his throat. "Actually, I'm not a family member, Doctor. I'll just wait outside." He started to rise.

"No, please stay, Constable," Jan's mother said, looking at him with pain in her eyes. She took Jan's hand and faced the doctor. "This is Grey's sister, January. How is he, Doctor?"

Jan sat stonily and listened to the litany of injuries her brother had sustained. It seemed to go on and on and with each item, Jan felt the iron fist squeezing her heart a little more. She realized Grey was lucky even to be alive. His many injuries were so life-threatening, it would be a while before they'd know for sure whether he'd make it, let alone be the same seventeen-year-old boy he had been.

"When can we see him?" Jan's mother asked.

"He still hasn't regained consciousness, but if you'll come with me, I'll take you to him."

Dr. Singh led Jan and her mother down the hall to a glass-fronted room filled with machines, multicoloured displays and an assortment of medical wizardry. The one piece of equipment Jan found the most frightening was the softly hissing ventilator. It had a plastic hose that ran directly from the machine to an incision in Grey's throat. Jan watched as the machine breathed for her brother.

14

*He's on life support. It's pretty bad.* The words kept running through her head.

She bit her lip to stop herself from crying. She knew this was going to break her mother's heart. He looked so damaged. Both his arms and hands were bandaged and one leg hung suspended from a traction device, but it was his head that shocked Jan. It was heavily swathed in gauze dressing; both Grey's eyes were swollen shut and his mouth had a jagged cut across one lip that had been sutured closed. There was tubing from the intravenous drips everywhere and one of them had six different bags and bottles of medication running.

Jan heard her mother's quick intake of breath when she saw her son. There was a nurse sitting near the bottom of his bed making notes on a chart. She glanced up when Jan and her mom entered the room. "Hello, I'm Dayna and I'll be Grey's primary nurse."

Jan cleared her throat. "I'm January Fournier, Grey's sister, and this is my mom, Violet Fournier." She looked at her brother, so still and pale.

The nurse smiled reassuringly at Jan and her mother.

Her mom nodded at the nurse, but her eyes never left her son's face. "How is he?" she asked quietly.

The nurse glanced at his chart. "He's stable, but his breathing is the big problem right now. His right lung had to be drained and it takes a while for the body to shake off the effects. Sometimes this prevents the immune system from rebounding like it should."

A look in the nurse's eyes told Jan everything her words hadn't. The truth was Grey wasn't responding to treatment the way they'd hoped and if he didn't soon, his chances of coming through this would be even slimmer.

The nurse saw Jan's mother looking at the array of machinery. "I know all this equipment is a little overwhelming." She put her pen down. "Mrs. Fournier,

Grey's condition is very serious. We're waiting for him to start responding to treatment, but he's still quite weak. The best thing for him to do now is just what he's doing, resting and letting his body begin the process of healing." Her mom nodded, understanding what was being said between the lines.

"Is there a chapel in the hospital?" Her mom's voice was clear and purposeful, but Jan heard the slight quaver in it.

"Yes there is, Mrs. Fournier."

Jan continued to stare at her brother as the nurse gave her mother directions to the chapel.

The nurse smiled at both Jan and her mother. "In case you can't sleep tonight and are wondering how things are going, please call and ask for me. I'll be able to tell you how Grey's progressing." It was obvious this nurse was well trained. She knew exactly what to say.

"Thank you, Dayna. I'll be in touch later." Violet Fournier turned and walked slowly out of her son's room.

As they left, Constable McKenna fell silently in step with them. Well over six feet tall, McKenna towered over both Jan and her mom. Glancing at her mom, Jan thought she looked very small and fragile. Her mom had never been a big woman, but somehow, in the hard fluorescent light of the sterile hallway, she appeared shrunken to Jan.

When they reached the double oak doors with the small brass sign saying simply CHAPEL, Jan stopped.

"Mom, I'll wait for you out here." She just didn't feel comfortable going in there.

Her mom looked like she was going to protest, then just nodded her head. She kissed Jan on the cheek, turned, and entered the sanctuary. David touched Jan's arm. "I'm going to go in and sit with your mother. She might want some company right now, even mine." He smiled reassuringly at her. "Will you be okay out here?" She could hear the concern in his voice.

"Sure, no problem. Oh, and David," she said. Now that her mom wasn't here, she could use his name without the implied breach of etiquette. "Try not to upset Mom any more than she is. I'm sure she doesn't know anything about the stolen bike either."

"Jan, your mom will have to be questioned about the theft," he sighed tiredly and nodded. "But not right now." He glanced in the direction of the chapel. "That's not my prime concern at this moment."

Jan watched him enter through the well-polished oak doors. She realized he was probably about the same age as her mother. Her mom had been only seventeen when she'd had Grey and Jan had come along a year later. She still looked young despite the old-fashioned way she dressed and wore her long black hair in coiled braids.

Jan was glad David had gone in to be with her mom. He was right, she would probably like some company, but Jan just couldn't bring herself to go into the chapel. She didn't think God would appreciate her asking a favour when she'd ignored Him up until now.

Jan sat and thought about the accident. How did Grey end up with a stolen bike? And not just any bike, that Bimota was worth big bucks. It was so rare; she'd only seen it in magazines. She knew Grey would never pass up a chance to ride a machine like that, but she was just as sure he'd never steal it just to go for a joy ride.

Somehow, she was going to have to find out what was going on. She needed to save Grey from going to jail, but more importantly, she needed to distract herself from her brother's struggle with life that was taking place just a few feet away.

# Chapter 2

The next morning, January woke early with a plan.

Her first step was to go to the police and convince them of Grey's innocence. At least try ... Then, she would invite them to help her find the real thief.

She was sure David McKenna thought Grey was innocent, despite how things looked. The problem would be convincing the rest of the Bragg Creek Police Department. If she could get to the officer investigating the thefts, she might be able to persuade him or her that Grey had nothing to do with the stolen bike, and hopefully, the police would then continue to look for the real thief.

Well, she decided, pushing back her snuggly down comforter and climbing out of bed, no time like the present. As she dressed she couldn't help feeling a little like David going to meet Goliath.

"Morning, Mom, any news?" she asked as she walked into the kitchen for breakfast. Her mom had taken some time off work to be with Grey. Jan thought it was nice having her home in the middle of the week. She just wished the reason were different.

"Good morning, honey. No, I called through the night and first thing this morning, but he's the same. I guess that might be considered a good thing. He's holding his own." Her mom walked to the sink and carefully rinsed out her favourite teacup, the one with the tiny pink roses on it, placing it gently in the cupboard. It was the one Grey had given her for Mother's Day three years ago.

Jan stopped in the middle of pouring her tea. "You mean he's still unconscious?" she asked, a little shocked.

Her mom nodded, unable to speak, and Jan could see her eyes cloud over with worry. Grey's unconsciousness, along with his breathing problems, had been a major concern to Grey's doctors. The trauma to his head had been significant, despite the fact Grey had worn his helmet. The good thing was, he *had* been wearing a helmet. The doctors said there was no doubt her brother would have died from the crash if he hadn't.

"And he's still on the ventilator?" Jan asked. Of all the miracle medicine her brother was receiving, somehow, it was the ventilator that bothered her the most. A small tremor ran down her spine when she thought of the machine that was breathing for her brother. She continued pouring her tea.

"Yes, but they think his breathing is improving a little. They're going to run some tests once he's a little stronger. I thought we could go in and see him this afternoon." Her mom smiled tiredly at her. "I was just on my way to Mass. Did you want to come?" she asked.

Jan looked at the ancient family bible lying on the kitchen table. It was so old, it was in Latin, but her mom still used it.

"Actually, Mom, I think I'll pass this time, but thanks for asking." Jan paused a moment, feeling awkward, then added, "Maybe you could light a candle for Grey from me."

Her mom looked at her with a raised eyebrow. Jan held up her hand to stop any comments. "I just believe in covering all the bases, Mom." She gulped the rest of her tea, then kissed her mom on the cheek as she headed out the door before any more religious discussion could be continued. "I'll meet you back here after lunch and we'll go see how Grey's doing."

David had explained the circumstances of Grey's accident to her mom as they'd left the hospital yesterday. He hadn't questioned her really, just filled her in on what was going on. Her mom had thought about this new revelation for a few moments, then said she knew her son had not stolen that bike and the police should look for another person. End of discussion.

* * *

Jan stopped by the town's small lending library to check old copies of the local paper for any items on bike thefts. Mrs. Cook, the librarian, ran the library like it was her personal fiefdom, but she turned out to be a great help. She knew just where to find any information about any topic in any edition of the local papers.

Jan was ushered into a small room that smelled of old books and newsprint and instructed to sit at a worn table in the corner. It was then that Mrs. Cook asked Jan what she needed and why.

As Jan explained, Mrs. Cook immediately began clucking her tongue and mumbling to herself about the town going to hell in a hand basket as she leafed through stacks of carefully catalogued newspapers. Soon, Jan had a pile of newspapers with a yellow Post-it on each one, indicating the page numbers pertaining to bike thefts. The librarian did all this with just a quick glance inside of each paper, as if confirming what she already knew. But in each case she was right.

The thefts started four months ago and so far, six bikes had been stolen, including the one Grey had crashed on.

Jan jotted down the names of the owners and the dates the bikes were stolen. A couple of the dates she specifically remembered being with Grey. She and Grey had been riding those days because he'd been helping her prepare to pass her motorcycle test. She wrote this down beside the days.

All the bikes were taken from wealthy locals when no one was at home, and so far there were no leads in the case, so the papers said. One article did mention that someone wearing black leathers and a fancy painted helmet was seen riding a big bike on West Bragg Creek Road at about the time of one of the thefts. However, it wasn't known if it was the stolen bike or just some tourist out for a ride. The article went on to say the police were continuing their investigation and hoped to have the case closed soon.

Obviously, if she were going to keep Grey from being paraded in the press as the prime suspect, she'd better get to the bottom of this fast.

Jan stuffed the sheet of paper with the names and dates of the thefts in her jacket and thanked Mrs. Cook for all her help. She then headed for the police station.

She parked her motorcycle in the parking lot and, after pulling her helmet off, actually tidied her unruly hair. She wanted to be taken seriously and helmet head was no way to make a first impression.

When she walked in, the lady officer working at the front desk looked up at her inquiringly.

"Can I help you, miss?" she asked in a businesslike tone.

"Ah, actually I'd like to speak to the officer in charge of the recent motorcycle thefts, please." She hoped her voice sounded confident and calm; she certainly didn't feel either.

The officer consulted a clipboard. "That would be Sergeant Gellar. Could I have your name, please."

Jan's stomach froze. Of all the policemen in Bragg Creek, why did it have to be Gellar? She felt her resolve start to melt. With his history with Grey, Gellar would never believe she wasn't just trying to get her guilty Métis brother off. This was bad, getting worse.

"Your name please, miss." The officer had her pencil poised over a message pad.

"It's January Fournier." At this, the officer hesitated just a fraction of a second, but Jan saw it. Obviously the case had already been discussed among staff.

"If you'll have a seat, Miss Fournier, I'll let Sergeant Gellar know you're here." She waited pointedly until Jan had sat on the bench opposite the desk, then picked up the phone and punched an extension number.

Jan watched as she explained who was waiting.

"He'll be with you shortly," the officer said as she replaced the receiver and returned to her paperwork.

Jan smiled and nodded in acknowledgement, then settled back to wait. The clock said 10:05. There were no magazines, so she contented herself with reading the array of posters on the wall.

By 11:45, she'd read all the posters twice, including the French translation, as well as bulletins, wanted posters and pictures of every missing kid from milk cartons across North America.

By this time the officer at the desk seemed to be wondering what the holdup was too. Jan had seen her surreptitiously checking the clock.

Jan had just made her mind up to ask the officer to call Sergeant Gellar again when David McKenna strode into the office.

"Jan, what are you doing here?" he asked, tossing his hat on the coat rack.

"Actually, I'm waiting to see Sergeant Gellar," she answered with a sigh. "But he seems to be really busy this morning."

"Is this about Grey? Maybe I can help," he said as he headed for the coffee machine. "Do you want one?" He held the pot up.

"No thanks to the coffee and maybe about Grey. Can we go somewhere and talk?"

"Sure, come into the *conference room*. That's a progressive way of saying *interrogation cell*." He grinned at her, then his mood became serious. "I didn't want to ask in front of the rest of the staff, but how's Grey. Any word?" he asked quietly as he ushered her into a side office.

"He's the same, still in a coma. Mom called this morning," Jan answered as she looked around the sparsely furnished room.

It had a long narrow table and four straight-backed chairs. That's all. She noticed the windows had thick metal mesh on them. The mesh, walls, furniture and door were all painted a flat battleship grey. Not an especially inviting room, she thought as she sat on one of the hard wooden chairs.

"And your mom? How's she holding up?" he asked, his voice softening.

"As well as could be expected, I guess. She's gone to Mass." Jan shook her head. "I hope she says a prayer for the doctors and nurses who're looking after Grey. They're the ones who are going to save him, not some magic man in the sky." She swiped at some imaginary dust on the tabletop.

David took a sip of his coffee, but said nothing. From the expression on his face, Jan suspected he'd figured out religion was a sore spot in the Fournier household.

He set his cup down thoughtfully. "You know your mom believes she's helping Grey. A lot of people would do exactly the same thing in her place."

"Yeah, well not me. I'm a little more hands on than Mom." It was getting too off topic for Jan; she steered the conversation back on track. "I'd like to know more about this stolen bike Grey crashed on. Where it came from, what the police are doing to find the real thief and if you've come up with any evidence to show Grey's innocent. You know he didn't take it, David." She looked defiantly at the constable, daring him to disagree.

Just then the door opened and Sergeant Gellar's tall, austere frame filled the doorway.

"I believe you were looking for me, Miss Fournier." His tone was stern and his words clipped.

"Yes," she stammered, momentarily taken aback. "I'm here about my brother, Grey. He was on a stolen bike yesterday when the accident occurred and I want to clarify things. My brother didn't steal that bike."

"That will be all, Constable," the sergeant said brusquely as he nodded at David.

"I know Grey, Sergeant. Maybe I could —" David began.

"That will be *all*, Constable McKenna." Sergeant Gellar stepped into the room.

David pushed himself up from the table. "Jan, please tell your mother I said hello." He left without further comment.

"Now, Miss Fournier, about your brother," Gellar began in that same cold tone. He placed a folder on the table and flipped through a couple of sheets. "According to protocol, I shouldn't even be talking to you about this case, but it's not inconceivable you may be an accomplice after the fact simply by not reporting your brother. A little talk may be in order."

He pulled a sheet of loose-leaf paper out of the folder. "Let's look at a few facts." His hawklike face looked smugly satisfied to Jan as he read the report. "Grey Fournier is a known juvenile offender who has been a troublemaker for some years now. He has a working knowledge of motorbikes and knows how much they could be fenced for, plus a valid license and is known for his love of speed on a bike." He paused for a second, then said, "As, I might add, do you." He glanced at her over the top of the sheet, then returned to reading. "The car dispatched yesterday was able to immediately confirm that the bike they were chasing did not belong to the suspect, but was, in fact, one reported stolen just two days before. It must have been just good luck the suspect crashed the same bike we were looking for."

He glanced icily at Jan. "The model of bike stolen was interesting in that our information about it says it was not just another fast bike. It was, in fact, one of only three of that make registered in Western Canada. This would have made the bike virtually impossible for your brother to sell. No fence would have touched anything that rare, too hard to get rid of. Not very smart, but then your people are not known for their astute judgement, are they?"

Jan bit back the answer she had waiting. She knew Gellar's type and her mom had taught her long ago, that there was no defending yourself against someone with a mind so closed, especially since he held the upper hand right now. She kept her face controlled and emotionless.

Gellar stared directly at her. "Not what you'd call an airtight case, but one the Crown will go ahead with, I'm sure." He replaced the sheet he'd been reading from into the folder.

"David, I mean Constable McKenna, didn't say Grey was being chased by the police yesterday when he crashed." She waited for him to explain.

Sergeant Gellar noisily straightened the papers in the folder. "Well, he wasn't actually being chased. We received a call about the accident, then proceeded from there."

Jan shook her head. "He may have had an accident while on a stolen bike, but I know my brother didn't steal that bike or any of these others." She pulled the scrap of paper with the information she'd received from the newspapers out of her pocket and put it on the table. "If you check the dates, I'm sure Grey will have an alibi for the times the bikes were stolen. I can vouch for two of the dates myself." She pushed the paper toward Gellar. A small quiver was trying to sneak into her voice, and she did her best to hide it.

He glanced at the paper. "I see you've been doing your homework. I suppose you and your brother have had enough time to concoct some sort of story to account for his time. You can't get your brother off that easily. This," he said, waving a hand at the paper, "is meaningless."

Jan grabbed the paper and stuffed it back into her coat, trying to keep calm.

Gellar went on, "Miss Fournier, the facts speak for themselves. However, we simply have to wait to see if this hypothesis is borne out. If the thefts cease now that your brother is hospitalized, then that's a pretty good indication of who the perpetrator was, wouldn't you agree?"

Jan didn't know what to say. He had a point.

"Now, if you've no other concrete evidence of your brother's innocence, I have a lot of *unfinished* cases which need my attention."

The dismissal in his voice was final. Jan didn't like the emphasis he'd put on *unfinished*. It implied he considered Grey's case already closed. Verdict in — the Métis kid was guilty. They always are.

Jan stood up, squaring her shoulders. "Thank you for your time, Sergeant," she said in her best imitation of her mother's calm voice. "I'll be back when I do have hard evidence, like the man who's actually stealing the bikes." She turned to leave, then stopped and faced him. "You know, my grandmother, who was Cree, once told me the Cheyenne have a saying, *Judge not by the eye but by the heart.* I know in my heart my brother's innocent."

"One more thing, Miss Fournier," Sergeant Geller added, his tone hard as flint. "This is a police matter. Leave it alone. I would hate to have to bring a charge of interfering with a police investigation." He paused, then added flatly, "But I will."

She turned and left the office with her head held up, keeping her hands in front of her body so he couldn't see how badly they were trembling.

In the parking lot she finally let herself take a deep, shaky breath. The first part of her plan hadn't exactly been a screaming success, but she would just have to work harder on part two. This was where she and the police caught the bad guy; Grey was cleared; and everyone lived happily ever after. Now it looked like she'd have to do it alone.

Pulling her motorcycle helmet on over her dark hair, she came to one inescapable conclusion. Sergeant Gellar believed he'd caught the right guy already and wasn't going to do any more looking for the real thief. However, one thing he'd said had hit home. If the thefts stopped in Bragg Creek, that was damning evidence Grey was guilty.

But what if whoever had set Grey up simply wanted a fall guy to take the heat off so the police would stop looking for him? All he'd have to do to remain safe was move his operation somewhere else.

The logical place was Calgary. It was only thirty-five minutes away, less on a bike, and because it was such a big city, any extra bike thefts would be lost in with the other crime statistics. However, there were a lot of police in Calgary, maybe some place like Banff, which got loads of tourists, but didn't have a large police department, would be a better target. She thought about which would give the best chance for a locally based bike thief.

But even if she figured out where he'd strike, how would she catch this guy? She needed to think clearly.

The one thing she found always blew the cobwebs from her head was a fast motorcycle ride up into the mountains. She started her bike, tightened her helmet and checked her fuel. She had time for a quick ride before meeting her mom.

Grey always kept her bike running way faster than the old clunker should. It made flashing down country roads a blast. She remembered how upset Grey had been the first time she'd beaten him on her bike. He seemed to forget it was he who'd tricked up the bike and given her the riding course. He'd always been really proud of his own riding abilities and she'd guessed it was bruised male pride that made him react that way. Even though it would mean a quarrel, she'd never *let* him win by throwing a race. That would have been worse.

Eventually, he came to accept the fact that his little sister could handle a bike ... really handle a bike and their relationship had gone to a new level. They not only loved one another as family, but also enjoyed the cama- raderie of being bike enthusiasts. They also respected one another's abilities. They'd never been as close as they were now.

She headed west, toward Kananaskis Country, climbing into the mountains on the twisting, curving road. The warm air, with its high-country summer smells, filtered into her helmet. She breathed in the intoxicating scent of pines and sun-warmed wildflowers.

She loved the way her bike felt when she leaned hard into a corner, hit the *sweet spot*, then brought it back up in a gracefully swaying duet — just her and the machine.

Her mind kept going over everything she knew about the case. Getting back copies of the local papers and looking for articles on the bike thefts had helped. However, there wasn't anything to tie the thefts together other than they were all in this general area. They all seemed so random. Perhaps a visit with her favourite police constable to enlist his help might be in order. She made a mental note to chat with David next time she saw him.

And then there was Bragg Creek itself. This was a small town. Someone would know something or have seen something and not even realized it was important. All she had to do was start people talking, then steer them onto the subject of motorbikes. The key to gathering information, and in the process clues, was to be a good listener. This was something she knew all about. In the restaurant, she was always overhearing conversations. People treated servers like they were invisible. It was a place to start.

As she drove, she thought once again of Grey. She wished he could be here with her on this awesome summer sunshine ride. Reluctantly, she turned her bike around and started back to meet her mom.

The ICU was extremely busy as Jan and her mother walked through the automatic doors.

Doctors and nurses moved with quick precision as they tended patients in varying degrees of distress. Everywhere there was the pervasive background noise of the machines. Machines for monitoring every vital function the human body had and with them alarms in the event that the responses didn't fall between parameters the machine deemed normal.

Machines for pumping fluids into bodies and machines for draining them back out. It was like some alien world of fantastic electronic wizardry. Yet, in contrast to these marvels of electro-tech hardware, were ordinary people struggling to simply stay alive.

Jan and her mother went directly to Grey's room. Jan expected the worst and was prepared for it.

The room was dimly lit and the soft sighing of the machines made a rhythmic sound, which could have been soothing, if you didn't know what they signified.

Jan walked to her brother's bedside. He looked so young, she thought as she looked down into his face. His heavily bandaged head lay against the white pillow for all the world as though he were just sleeping, not deep in a coma from which he might never return.

Her mom picked up one of his hands. Jan, on the other side of the bed, could see the strain on her face.

Jan cleared her throat. "You know they say a person in a coma can hear you when you talk to them. Maybe we should try that. It could help him come back." She slipped her fingers around Grey's other hand and squeezed gently. "You know how opinionated Grey is and I'm sure he'll want to put his two cents into any discussion we have." She smiled at her brother's still face. "Isn't that right, Grey?"

Her mom picked up right away. "I don't want you two arguing about anything here in the hospital. You both behave."

That started a conversation that covered any and all topics Jan and her mom could think of. They discussed the weather, sports, new hairdos, clothes, Jan's bike, her mom's car — anything, just so Grey could hear the sound of their voices.

They'd just finished a lively discussion on whether or not they should get a puppy and if they did what breed and who would look after it, when Dr. Singh came into the room.

"I hear from the nurses there's quite the discussion going on in here." He smiled at January and her mom. "And as per usual, the man can't get a word in edgewise." He spoke quietly, but something in his voice made Jan feel reassured.

"We were hoping it might help, Doctor," Jan's mom said by way of explanation.

"It's a very good idea, Mrs. Fournier," he said with a nod. "We honestly don't know how much a coma patient picks up from his environment. But it's always good to assume the patient is coming out of, not going deeper into the coma. Your voices might be just the stimulus he needs to struggle to the surface."

The idea Grey had to struggle to the surface at all was a little unsettling, but Jan hoped it wasn't too great a distance for her brother.

"How's he doing, Doctor?" her mom asked in her calm, low voice.

"Why don't we step outside and discuss this, Mrs. Fournier," he said as he checked Grey's pupils with a small pencil light.

"Certainly." She leaned over and kissed Grey on the cheek. "Good bye, sweetheart, I'll be back tomorrow."

Jan squeezed her brother's hand. "We can finish this business about who cleans up after our new puppy tomorrow," she said cheerily.

Once they were out of Grey's room, the doctor's face became very serious. "I won't lie to you two," he said and Jan knew she wasn't going to like what came next. "The longer Grey is in that coma, the more chance of permanent damage. The added complication of his need for respiratory assistance is a further warning sign." He shook his head. "I wish I could be more encouraging, but at this point, things could still go either way. I want you to be aware of all the eventualities."

Her mother nodded. "Thank you for being so honest with us, Doctor, but you needn't worry. Grey will come through this." She smiled. "Have faith, we have some powerful players on our side." The doctor nodded, and gave her arm a little squeeze.

Together, Jan and her mom left the hospital, neither one saying much. Once they were in the car, her mom took a deep breath.

"We can't let ourselves become negative, January. We must be positive and ..."

Jan gave her mom a weak smile. "I know, Mom, and have faith." She knew her mom was right, and Jan did have faith. The difference between her and her mom was Jan had faith in Grey's will to live and the doctor's modern technological miracles. She couldn't bring herself to think some all-knowing being would intercede with death on her brother's behalf. Maybe her mom was right after all; you had to have faith and each person's faith was his or her own.

They rode in companionable silence for a while, but Jan felt better. She sighed and looked out the window.

The one thing she was sure of was the need for her to clear Grey. She couldn't believe her brother had stolen that bike, but she needed proof.

It was then that it happened. They'd just turned off the main highway on the Bragg Creek exit, when out of nowhere, a very fast motorcycle suddenly careened past, cutting them off. And from the way he nearly clipped their front fender, but avoided any actual contact, Jan could have sworn the guy did it on purpose. Almost like he was showing off.

Her mom swerved the car to avoid hitting the rider, coming dangerously close to the edge of the road.

Jan grabbed for the armrest as her mom fought to bring the car back under control. She could feel the tires slipping off the pavement and onto the shoulder. The ditch was next and maybe a rollover.

Out of the corner of her eye, January caught a blurred glimpse of the bike and rider as he sped by. He was dressed all in black leathers and was on a new green, white and black Ninja. The bike was leaned over hard as he took the corner. This guy could really ride!

Finally, her mom pulled the car to a stop at the side of the road. Jan could see she was shaking, but whether it was from fear or anger, she couldn't tell.

"Did you see that? A lunatic like that should have his license taken away!" her mom said angrily. Her knuckles were white as she still gripped the wheel tightly.

Jan watched as the bike quickly disappeared down the road. She hadn't been able to get a look at his face through the tinted visor, but she had seen a symbol painted on his black Shoei helmet. It had been very distinctive — the jagged slash of a shiny silver lightning bolt.

# Chapter 3

Jan's mom was still trying to calm down from the incident with the bike even after they reached home. From the expert way the guy rode, Jan knew they were in no real danger of his hitting them unless her mom had reacted wrong. Fortunately, she'd done the right thing, avoiding the bike the only safe way she could. There were always a lot of motorbikes on that road and not all of them were courteous riders, some were hot-doggers.

At any other time, Jan would have simply admired the way the guy could ride, but it had been bad timing coming so close to Grey's accident. The rider with the really wild insignia on his helmet had been heading for Bragg Creek, but Jan didn't know anyone around here who owned a new Ninja or who could ride like that.

Jan had learned Sergeant Gellar had stopped by to interview her mom about Grey's involvement with the stolen bike. Her mom had taken it calmly and tried to cooperate, but she'd made it perfectly clear to him that Grey had nothing to do with any theft.

Grey still hadn't been formally charged, and hopefully, Jan would be able to clear his name before Sergeant Gellar put any more wheels in motion.

Jan wanted to talk with David McKenna. He had inside information no one else would have and if he felt like sharing it with her ... Well, she wasn't going to say no. She called the police office and left a message for David, then went to change for her shift, which started at five o'clock.

Jan exchanged the usual pleasantries with the day waitress, then got busy. The small town information net had already spread the news about Grey's accident and lots of locals stopped by to ask how he was doing. The good part of this was as they asked about Grey, she asked them questions also — about the rash of stolen bikes and whether they'd noticed any strangers in town. No one seemed to have seen anything. There was one common element to the robberies, however. They always occurred when the owners weren't home, sometimes at odd hours, like the middle of the day. Coincidence or good planning, Jan wondered.

She'd just finished explaining Grey's condition for the twentieth time, when David McKenna walked through the restaurant door. He nodded at Jan, then went straight to the staff table and sat down.

"Just coffee, David?" Jan asked as she filled a cup for him.

"First things first, Jan. How's your brother?" he asked in a concerned voice.

"The same, but we're hoping for some good news soon." She tried to smile at David, but it didn't turn out very convincing. "Real soon."

"Grey's a strong kid, he's going to come through this," he said encouragingly. "I was a little worried when I got your message at the cop shop, but I figured if it were something urgent, you'd have had me contacted. You can do that Jan, anytime, you understand?"

Jan nodded; she knew what he meant.

"Good." He smiled at her. "Now about supper. How about one of those great Buffalo Burgers and fries?" he said, reaching for the coffee.

"Sounds good to me," Jan answered, smiling as she jotted the order down.

She headed for the kitchen.

"One Buff Burg for the good constable, Josh, with fries." She slid the order into the wicket.

"Right," Josh said, heading for the freezer where the meat was kept.

Jan finished cleaning the tables as the restaurant emptied. The supper rush was over, and on a weeknight, that just about did it for customers.

"Order up!" came the call from the kitchen. Jan delivered David's order, then grabbed a coffee and sat with him as he ate his meal.

"Sergeant Gellar thinks Grey did the bike thefts, and he's planning on putting him away for good this time," she said without preamble.

David took a drink of his coffee before he said anything. "Where did you get that idea?"

"The little conversation he had with me and the one he had with Mom. Now, about the bike thefts ..." She ladled sugar into her cup, added milk, then popped in two straws, which she liked to use when she drank coffee.

"I don't think it's a good idea to discuss an ongoing case." He picked up a fork and let it hover over his fries. "Do you have any malt vinegar for these?"

Jan retrieved the vinegar from the cabinet and returned to her coffee. "Grey hasn't been charged — yet. Therefore it's not a *case* and I'm just a concerned citizen whose brother is about to be shafted by a bigoted rednecked southern sheriff." She set her cup down rather hard. A little spilt over the edge and she reached for a napkin to clean it up.

Just then the door opened and Collin Watson strode in. He walked over to Jan before she could get up. Pulling out one of the chairs from an adjoining table, he spun it around and sat down with his arms draped over the back.

He nodded at David, then turned to Jan.

"I'm here to pick up my dad's poker night pizzas. I trust they're ready?" It was almost a challenge.

Jan didn't let on she'd forgotten about the standing order for pizza on Mr. Watson's poker nights. She just hoped Josh had remembered.

"I'm sure they are. I'll just go check." She got up and headed for the kitchen.

"Josh, Collin's here for his dad's poker order. Please tell me you remembered." She made a face. "It's always the same — a personal-sized Greek for Mr. Lockington, a veggie for Mr. Walker, a Hawaiian for Mr. Meering and a pepp/mush for Mr. McMaster, oh, and a Bragg Special for Collin's dad, unless one of the regulars is away, then you double up on the Bragg because Collin sits in," she said in a singsong voice as she recited the litany all in one breath. She shrugged. "With everything that's been happening, it just went out of my head."

Josh just stood and listened to her, then slowly shook his head and walked to the back of the kitchen. He returned with an armful of boxes that smelled tantalizingly as though they contained a delightful selection of homemade pizzas. He held the boxes out to her.

She grinned at him. "Josh, you're wonderful — a real lifesaver. If I had to apologize to Collin for screwing up the order, I'd have choked. Thanks, I owe you one." She thought he looked a little embarrassed at her enthusiastic praise.

She carried the pizzas out and set them on a table, then took the money Collin held out and went back to the kitchen to clear the bill.

He was still sitting at the staff table when Jan returned with his change.

"Keep it," he said indicating the change. "Oh, and I'm supposed to pass on a message. My dad heard about Grey. He thinks it would make a great pro bono case. You know, he'll do it for the love of justice."

Jan was too surprised to say anything.

Collin grinned at her and Jan could see why the girls flocked around him. With his blue eyes and blonde good looks, he should have had some California address, like Hollywood and Vine, not Bragg Creek.

Finally, she regained her voice. "Gee, Collin, that's awfully nice of your dad," she said, trying not to sound sarcastic, "but Grey hasn't been charged with anything, yet. How did he hear about Grey anyway?"

"Actually, my dad's pretty tight with Sergeant Gellar and I guess he must have mentioned it to him," he answered as a casual explanation.

"So much for confidentiality," Jan said ruefully.

"Hey, my dad's a wicked lawyer." Collin paused for a moment, then a sly grin spread across his beach-boy face. "Besides, I think he's planning on running for some kind of political office this fall and it looks good to defend some poor, downtrodden minority who's caught up in the wheels of justice. Even if he does lose, he'll still look like a hero — fighting Big Brother for the underdogs."

"I always thought being on the side of the innocent was enough," Jan said pointedly.

Collin shrugged his shoulders and smiled disarmingly, then stood up and swung the chair back in place. "Well, I'd better get the grub back. I'm sitting in for Mr. McMaster tonight, and the guys are waiting to take his money." He laughed. "When Gerry Meering was away and I sat in, I made him sixty bucks and good old Gerry let me keep the winnings. Dad says it's not fair because

38

he's away so rarely, he has very few chances of me winning any money for him." He grabbed the pizzas and sauntered to the door.

"Give me hand with this stupid door, will you, Jan?" he asked, holding the pizzas out to her. "I've got a full house here." He laughed at his joke.

She sighed and went to get the door for him.

Jan watched him put the pizzas on the passenger seat in his car. She was just going to turn away, when she spotted Sergeant Gellar walking up to Collin's car.

She wondered if he was going to give Collin a ticket for parking in the handicap stall in front. Jan smiled. That would be nice. Instead, Gellar and Collin seemed to be discussing the merits of Collin's car. Both were laughing and talking like old buddies. Jan turned away in disgust. It looked like it wasn't only Collin's dad who was tight with Gellar.

She walked back to the staff table and dropped back into her chair. "I'm sure Grey will be thrilled to be considered a *poor minority*," she said.

"One thing he was right about, Jan: his dad is a good lawyer." David reached for his coffee. "He's been getting Collin out of tight squeezes for years. His motives might be suspect, but he is a good man to have on Grey's side."

Josh came out of the kitchen and sat down beside Jan. "What did Golden Boy want? A bulk discount on his pizza order?" He sipped on his glass of cold water.

Jan giggled. "Not quite. He was letting me know his dad is offering some help for Grey."

She glanced at today's T-shirt, which said *Rodeo RAW 'cause chicks dig scars and bones heal!* Normally, she hated all that macho cowboy stuff, but on Josh it looked good. Her eyes were drawn to his hands, which, she noticed, were scrubbed meticulously clean. This

39

only made the calluses more noticeable against his sun-tanned skin. Jan couldn't remember ever seeing Josh when he didn't look tanned. It was probably from working outside year round in all kinds of weather.

Shaking his head, Josh went on disgustedly, "If it weren't for his dad, Collin Watson would have been in jail a long time ago. That pot bust alone last year should have ended him up inside." He shrugged his shoulders, then changed the subject. "I haven't had a chance to talk to you much tonight. How's Grey doing anyway?" Josh asked, sounding genuinely interested.

"He's pretty busted up, but we hope he's improving. He's not conscious yet and they still have him on a ventilator to help with his breathing." She busied herself stirring the last of her coffee with the straws.

"He's going to make it though, isn't he?" Josh looked at her.

"That's the plan," Jan said brightly, but she could feel the tears starting. She changed the subject. "Speaking of bikes, some crazy cut Mom and me off today, almost put us in the ditch. You can tell it's summer by the number of bikes on the road, not all being driven courteously, I might add."

David was instantly interested. "Did you see who it was?"

"No, it was just at the turnoff where the highway from Banff meets Bragg Creek Road. The guy was going like a bat out of hell on a brand-new green, white and black Ninja. He had on black leathers and his helmet had a dark visor so I couldn't see his face. I didn't recognize the bike as local. I guess he was from Banff."

"Can you think of anything else, Jan, like part of the plate number or distinguishing marks?" Constable McKenna had turned into a cop again.

Jan thought for a minute. "There was one thing. He had this really funky symbol on his helmet. A silver lightning bolt ran down the sides. It really stood out on the black helmet."

"What time was this?" David asked.

"About four o'clock, maybe a little after. Why?" She knew this was real police questioning, not just idle curiosity.

"I was doing a little checking of my own today. It seems the Banff police had a brand-new Ninja ZX11 with the same paint scheme reported stolen early this afternoon. The owner said he saw a guy wearing dark leathers and a helmet with a fancy motif hanging around the parking garage as he was leaving his bike."

Jan looked at him. "Hey, wait a minute, didn't the papers say our thief wore black leathers and a helmet with a design also? It sounds like it could be the same guy." Her mind connected the dots, and came up with a picture. "This means the bike thefts are still going on, just not here. This is great! It means my big brother is off the hook." This was the break she needed.

Excited at what this meant for Grey, she impulsively hugged Josh, who'd been quietly listening. "This is super!" she said, delighted at the prospect of Grey being cleared. Then she realized what she'd just done. "Oh, sorry, Josh. I just got carried away."

"Wait a minute," David went on. "All this means is bikes are being stolen. It doesn't mean the thefts are connected. Don't get your hopes up, Jan. It could be purely coincidence."

"I don't believe in coincidence, David, and as a good cop, neither should you. The guy who ran my mom and me off the road today is our man." She pushed her empty coffee cup away and sat back in her chair.

"You're not listening, Jan." But she was already miles ahead of David.

41

"We have to come up with a plan to catch this guy." She looked at David for confirmation.

"If, and I do mean *if*, this guy is connected to our thefts, it becomes a police matter instantly. The Banff RCMP are already on this. I may need you to give me a formal statement, Jan, so please don't discuss the incident with anyone else."

"David, you have to help me with this. You know Gellar will just think it's the Métis kid's half-breed sister trying to get him off," she said angrily.

David looked at her as though he were going to say something in Sergeant Gellar's defence, then his face softened. "Don't worry. I'm not giving up on Grey just yet." He smiled at her. "Or his sister."

He left some bills on the table and started to leave. "Great burger, Josh." Then he stopped and turned to Jan. "Maybe I'll just swing by your place and have a little talk with your mom about the incident, in case she remembers something you missed." He gave her a warning look. "And remember Jan, this is police business." He left the restaurant.

Jan was sure it was David who had called her mother late last night. She could tell from the way her mother's voice changed when she spoke to him.

"This is really something," Josh said, putting his empty glass back on the table. He coughed a couple of times, then, reaching into his back pocket, withdrew a small blue plastic vial. He placed one end in his mouth and sprayed some as he inhaled.

Noticing Jan staring at him, he slipped the cap back on the inhaler and tucked it away again. "Ventolin, I have asthma," he said in a raspy voice. "Had it all my life. It's a royal pain because I work with livestock so much, it seems like I'm always wheezy."

"I had no idea," Jan said amazed. One thing was for sure — Josh was no complainer.

He continued, "Since graduating from school this year, all I can think about is how I'd like to leave here and travel the world. I want to go somewhere where they've never heard of heifers, horses or hay."

Jan wasn't used to hearing such personal talk from Josh. It was strange, but she liked it.

He turned to look at her. "Do you really think you can catch this guy? How will you go about baiting the trap?" He seemed really interested. Then he added, "If there's anything I can do to help, I want you to know I'm here for you. In fact, I'd really like to help you find him."

Jan was so surprised at his offer, she didn't know what to say. "Ah, yeah, sure," she finally stammered. This was something she hadn't expected. Maybe having some help would get Grey cleared sooner. It would be so nice to have someone she could talk to, besides her mom and David. They were, after all, really old adults.

She smiled at Josh. "You know, I'd like that. I really would. Thanks for the offer." She thought a moment. "The first thing I have to do is find out from the people who had bikes taken from this area, if they remember seeing a guy with a lightning bolt helmet snooping around before their bikes went missing."

"I can help with that. Two of the thefts happened down the road from us. I'll talk to them," Josh offered.

"And I'll check with David on the other cases to see if anyone remembered anything."

Jan felt great as she and Josh finished their shift. The freak on the bike may be just the break she'd needed, and Josh had been so unexpectedly nice. In fact, he'd been friendlier to her than he'd ever been before. She felt flattered for some reason. It wasn't as though she were a damsel in distress and Josh had ridden in on his white horse or anything. Not quite, but it was nice anyway. She was seeing Josh Blakeman in a whole new light.

She finished cleaning up and prepared to leave. Josh had been on the phone when she'd looked into the kitchen a couple of minutes earlier, probably someone looking for a takeout pizza order. People here thought the posted hours of operation were merely a guideline.

She dawdled just a little more than she really had to before going in to say goodnight. He looked up as she entered the kitchen.

"I'm about set to go. I'll see you tomorrow," she said casually.

"Yeah, this is a rap for me, too," he said, grabbing his gear and switching off the kitchen light.

"Where are you parked?" she asked, nodding at his motorcycle helmet.

"Ol' Lucifer's on the far side of the lot."

She smiled. "Hey, me too. I don't suppose I could ask you a favour. It is pretty late. Could you wait until my bike's started before you leave, just in case the darn thing won't go."

Okay, that was a little white lie. She knew her bike would start, but he had been awfully nice and, she noticed yet again just how cute he was. She smiled at him. "I'd hate to be stranded in the parking lot at this hour."

"Sure, no problem," Josh said, turning off the rest of the restaurant lights.

When they stepped outside, Jan thought it seemed unusually dark out. There must be no moon, she decided as she waited while Josh hurriedly fumbled with the lock on the troublesome outer door.

"Robin should replace the whole door, including that old lock," Jan said as she watched. They started across the deserted parking lot.

"Is Grey going to be able to tell us where he got the bike, Jan?" Josh asked. "It could be the guy with the helmet."

Jan decided to confide in Josh. "I would have asked him today, but he's still in a coma. Josh, they're not even sure he'll come out of it again. They haven't said so in those words, but I know what they mean with all that slick talk."

She kicked at a small rock. "To tell you the truth, I feel like it might be partly my fault. Ever since I got my license, it was a standing joke that I would be a better rider than he is one day. Grey always scoffed at the idea of his kid sister actually being able to outdo him on a bike, but lately, when we race, I've been beating him and outcornering him and little things like that. Maybe Grey took that big bike to prove something to himself, like he was still on top. Maybe, if I hadn't been so gung ho on beating him, he wouldn't have pushed that Bimota so hard and crashed." She could feel the tears starting, but she couldn't help it. What if it was true?

Josh stopped and looked at her.

"It's not your fault, Jan. Grey lost control of a really fast bike he couldn't handle. It happens. You shouldn't beat yourself up about it."

She nodded mutely, his words cutting through the cloud of guilt that had been building up in the back of her mind.

He suddenly smiled at her, and Jan thought his whole face seemed to change. It seemed to soften somehow.

"Good, I'm glad that's straight." He changed the subject. "That bike cutting you off today was really interesting. But I guess there are a lot of bikes like that one. Do you really think they'll be able to tie the guy into the thefts? McKenna seemed real interested."

Jan thought about it. "I think this Lightning Rider is the bike thief. The chances of there being two guys with that description are too remote. He's our man, all right. It will just take the police a little longer to come to the same conclusion." She smiled weakly at Josh.

Josh stopped and looking back at the restaurant, frowned. "Jeez, I forgot to check whether the door's really locked. I'd better go rattle it to make sure. Robin would have a stroke if she comes in tomorrow and the door's not locked. Wait here, I'll just be a minute." He left her standing in the middle of the parking lot as he headed back to the restaurant.

Jan felt better now that she'd told Josh about her visit with Grey. That had really upset her, more than she'd let on. She watched as he loped across the parking lot. He was tall and slim, but he moved easily, almost gracefully.

With a warm shock, she realized she and Josh had been talking, really talking, like a boyfriend and girlfriend would talk. His sudden friendliness was just what she needed right now. Maybe he'd just been waiting for an excuse to get closer to her; after all, she was one of a very few people who got along with him. He was not a joiner and didn't hang out with any particular group. Also, between school, the ranch and the restaurant, he hadn't had much chance to do the social thing like Collin.

The thought of Collin Watson gave her a twinge of annoyance. He was a real treat. Ever since the shoplifting, Jan hadn't liked or trusted the guy. He was constantly in trouble, but always seemed to squeak out of it. And that offer his dad had made! When Mom hears about that, she's going to hit the roof.

Josh strode back toward her. "Hey, Jan, I was wondering, do you want to go for a short ride before going home?" he asked with that same appealing grin.

"My mom's expecting me, I don't think ..." she stammered, starting to refuse him, but the look on his face melted any resolve she might have been pretending to have. She gave him a conspiratorial look. "You know, if we swing by my place first, I can tell her where we're going and when I'll be back. I just don't want to add to her worries right now."

Josh nodded. "Sounds like a plan to me."

They started walking toward their bikes. Jan felt foolishly happy. After all, he could be just taking pity on her because of Grey. Maybe, maybe not, she smiled to herself.

When they reached her house, Jan went in to talk to her mom, while Josh waited outside.

"The hospital called," Jan's mom said as soon as Jan opened the door.

Jan's stomach tightened. "Is Grey all right?" she asked apprehensively.

Her mom smiled, and relief flooded through Jan.

"They took him off the ventilator today and he did fine. He can breathe on his own." She hugged Jan. "Isn't this great news?"

Jan felt like a heavy weight had been lightened. No more ventilator. Yes!

"Does this mean he's coming out of his coma?" she asked hopefully.

"The doctors wouldn't go that far, but they were very encouraged by this development." Her mother stopped, suddenly realizing that Jan still had her helmet with her and her boots on.

"Were you planning on going somewhere?" she asked.

Jan quickly explained what she wanted to do.

Her mom hesitated, not sure if it was a good idea for her sixteen-year-old daughter to go for a late-night ride with a boy. But she'd relented when Jan had laughingly added not to worry, there were no back seats on motorbikes.

Jan hugged her mom, promising not to be late, then hurried out to tell Josh the good news about her brother.

"That's great, Jan," he said, grinning at her. "I guess this calls for a celebration."

"You bet! Let's go," she said, yanking her helmet down over her head.

She pulled the manual choke on and kicked over the motor on her Yamaha RZ-350. It barked quickly to life with a sound that was sharp and crisp.

Josh, who'd been leaning against his bike waiting for her, swung his leg over his '79 Honda CMT 400. Pulling on the choke, he hit the electric start. The starter whined, but the motor refused to catch. He kept trying until the smell of gasoline filled the air. "Seems Ol' Lucifer isn't too keen on the idea. We just have to give the carburetor a minute to clear."

"You know, Josh, it just might be time to put Ol' Lucifer out to pasture. Have you ever thought about a newer bike?" she asked.

"Careful what you say in front of him, Jan. He's cantankerous enough without thinking I'm going to re-tire him. If he takes it into his head to act up, we might not get that ride." He grinned at her.

"Seriously, Josh, you're going to start having real problems with that thing soon and I'd hate to think of you spending your hard-earned money buying a new hat for an old horse."

Josh seemed to think that over for a moment.

"New hat for an old horse, huh?" he chuckled. "You may be on to something." He tried the starter again and finally, the old bike coughed and caught.

He nodded to Jan, who flipped the visor down on her helmet and tapped her bike into first gear with her foot.

The bike responded quickly to the throttle as she headed down the driveway and out onto the road. Josh tucked in behind her.

The night wind was warm and soft. They'd headed past the old Trading Post store at the far south edge of town. Here the road twisted and turned and lent itself to practising cornering and apexes. Jan was always trying to hone her skills on her bike.

She noticed Josh handled his bike pretty well, in fact with a little coaching like she'd received at the motorcycle school, she was sure he could become a really great rider.

When they finally returned home, Jan felt relaxed and ready to take on the world.

She pulled her bike up to the garage and shut off the engine. Josh pulled in behind her and turned his bike around so it was pointing back down the driveway.

She pulled off her helmet and pushed her hair back. "That was a lot of fun Josh, thanks," she said and genuinely meant it.

"I'm just glad me and my buddy here," he said, patting the tank on his bike, "could be of help." His tone became more serious. "And Jan, if you want to talk about Grey's case or need some leads tracked down, call me. As a matter of fact, this old cowboy brain might be able to give you a new slant on things. Just let me know what you find and we'll work on it together." He reached out and ruffled her hair. "Nice helmet head, Fournier. See you at work." Then, revving the engine, he drove down the driveway and into the night.

Jan watched him go, waving as he drove away. This had been a fantastic evening — first the super news about Grey and then this. Wow.

# Chapter 4

When David McKenna called the next day, Jan thought he wanted to speak to her, but was surprised when he asked for her mom.

"Mom, Constable McKenna wants to talk to you," she called to her mom, who was upstairs.

"I'll get it up here," her mom answered as she picked up the extension. Jan heard her mom's cheery hello as she quietly replaced the receiver.

As she went back to the living room couch and the book she'd left, Jan wondered whether something had come up about Grey's case. It just wasn't fair. Grey was fighting for his life and even when he recovered, he may have to fight for his life again — in court. Jan knew it would finish Grey if he were sent to prison.

Her mom came downstairs a few minutes later and Jan noticed she'd changed into a pretty flower-print dress. "Jan, Constable McKenna is going to take us to the hospital today. He has some errands in the city and offered to drive us. I think he's worried about Grey. He really likes you kids." She smiled at Jan.

Her mom bustled about the living room doing busy work.

Jan watched her for a minute. Something was up; her mom was definitely huffling. Huffling was the term she and Grey used for this busy work when their mom would go around the room straightening things that didn't need straightening and dusting things that didn't need dusting.

"Is there something on your mind, Mom?" Jan finally asked.

"Me?" her mom said, surprised, in the middle of fluffing a pillow. "No, not really, dear." She hesitated, then stopped what she was doing and walked over to Jan. Sitting on the couch next to her daughter, she folded her hands in her lap. "Actually, to be perfectly honest, yes, there is something on my mind. I'm a little concerned about your brother's recovery. His still being in a coma is a little ... worrisome." She chose her words very carefully.

Jan slowly closed the book she'd been reading. It was an interesting one about some woman who'd touched an ancient gravestone and been instantly transported back in time. She liked it because they hadn't cheated on the time travel problem, the one where you always wondered why, if the hero could move through time, he didn't just go back a day before the terrible thing happened and prevent it, instead of trying to fix it after. She'd decided there should be some rules governing the writing of time-travel novels.

Jan faced her mom, took a deep breath and exhaled. "Mom, you have no idea how much better that makes me feel. I've been worried sick and didn't want to say anything in case I upset you." She smiled and felt her lip quiver. "All I can think about is Grey still being in that coma. Lying there, hour after hour, and us not knowing whether he will come out of it or not. I even felt guilty because he'd been in the crash, like it was somehow my fault."

Her mom hugged her. "Oh Jan, you mustn't feel that way. It was no one's fault. It was an accident." She thought a moment. "It's extremely stressful when someone you love is so desperately ill, but I think it really helps if we talk about it. Left alone, the imagination can come up with some very strange ideas. I think it's only natural in a situation like this, to feel some irrational guilt because he's lying there, and you're not. Maybe it's because we're helpless bystanders and doing nothing is the hardest job of all." She smiled at Jan, both of them feeling better. "Now, how about a quick cup of tea?"

Jan nodded and smiled at her mom. She was right.

* * *

When they arrived at the hospital, they went directly to Grey's room. Dayna, his nurse, smiled as they came in.

"His vitals are fine. In fact, his breathing is coming along better than we'd hoped. It means his lungs are recovering from the initial trauma." She nodded at Jan and her mom. "That's a good sign."

"Any indication he's coming out of the coma?" her mom asked. Her voice was almost a whisper.

Dayna put her pen down on top of the chart she was working on. "No, nothing yet," she said sympathetically. "But we're hoping for improvement as he heals and his other injuries present less stress on his systems."

Jan swallowed; all she'd heard was no, her brother was still on the edge.

David, who'd been standing quietly behind her mom, moved to Grey's bedside table. "I hope you don't mind," he said, looking at her mother, "I knew your relatives were Cree from Hobbema, so I drove out and talked to your uncle." He could see the surprise on her face. "It was a little," he searched for the right word, "forward of me, but it was important. He sent this in for Grey. He thought it might help."

With that, David reached into a small leather bag he'd been carrying and took out a long piece of braided grass. "It's blessed sweetgrass," he explained to the nurse, who had a puzzled look on her face. "It's part of the spiritual beliefs of Native peoples. It's used in a smudge for cleansing the spirit and to support healing." When she still looked unclear, he went on, "Additional help, sort of like incense in the church." He saw understanding dawn on the nurse's face.

David smiled. "I know we can't burn it in here," he said, nodding at the oxygen equipment, "but I think it might be a good thing to have right now."

Usually Jan's mom was a very private person, who kept her business to herself, so Jan was really surprised when she saw the thanks and appreciation in her mother's eyes as she nodded. David McKenna must have gone up a big notch in her mom's book to let him do something so personal, and he'd gone up several in Jan's.

She watched him lay the braid of sweetgrass on the table. For some reason, Jan suddenly felt everything was going to be okay.

* * *

Later that evening, Josh listened as Jan told him about the events at the hospital.

"... and now, I just think everything is going to work out. And my mom, wow, if you'd have asked me what her reaction to something like that would have been, I'd have bet money it wasn't what actually happened. I thought she'd by angry at David, who's not a relative,

53

for getting the sweetgrass, but instead, he's like some kind of family hero."

She looked at Josh and smiled. They were walking along the covered wooden boardwalk that connected all the small shops in the mall. Their shift had been extremely busy and Jan had made nearly forty dollars in tips. The whole place was deserted now, but she liked the peace and quiet as they walked toward their bikes. The warm July night seemed to enfold them with soft scented air.

" The doctors think he's going to make it, don't they?" Josh asked as he sat on an old wooden bench that was outside the candy shop.

"They're guardedly optimistic, which is doctor lingo for he's doing a little better, but he's not out of the woods yet." Jan dropped onto the bench beside him.

Just then a couple of cowboys exited noisily from the Powderhorn Saloon and started down the boardwalk. They were laughing and jostling one another as they came toward Josh and Jan.

Josh glanced at the boisterous men, then stood up and began to walk to his bike, leaving Jan sitting on the bench. "Josh, wait up!" she called, but he'd pulled his helmet on and couldn't hear her.

The two cowboys, who'd obviously been in the saloon for some time, pushed clumsily by her, apologizing by doffing their dusty cowboy hats. "'Scuse me ma'am," they slurred as they passed. Jan nodded at them as she started after Josh.

She'd just reached the top of the stairs which led off the boardwalk and into the parking lot, when she glanced at a poster stapled to the wooden support pillar that held up the roof. Stopping, she stared at the brightly coloured sheet of paper.

She waved at Josh, who was already on his bike. He started it up and drove over to her.

"I've got to get going, Jan," he said, blipping the throttle a little to keep the old bike from stalling.

"Josh, did you see this?" she asked excitedly, pointing to the fluorescent pink-coloured paper.

Josh looked up at the poster and read the bold print. *The Banff Rocky Mountain Centre presents the Third Annual International Motorbike Show and Sale.*

"It's this weekend," Jan said excitedly. "This is the perfect bait! Every bike enthusiast within riding distance will be there. The pickings will be too choice for our Lightning Bolt guy not to make a grab." She thought a moment. "I'll tell Robin I can't work on Saturday, then bike up to Banff and see if I can find this guy."

"Do you think that's a good idea, Jan? I know I won't be able to ditch work, so I can't go with you and going alone isn't the safest idea," he said. "Maybe you should just leave it to the cops. Besides," he added, "the guy may not even show up."

"Are you kidding?" Jan scoffed. "He'll be there. He feels safe now that Grey is taking the heat. He thinks he's outsmarted the cops and is home free." She shook her head. "However, I'm not going to tell anyone, especially David McKenna. With all his new personal interest in the Fourniers, he'd freak and tell me to stay out of police business, but there's no way I'm leaving this to the likes of Gellar to look into."

"At least promise me one thing," Josh said seriously.

"Sure, as long as it doesn't stop me from catching this guy," she answered.

"Go directly to the Banff Centre and wait. I know that place. You can park your bike under the trees on the south side of the parking lot and watch from there. If this guy's from around here, he may recognize your bike and get suspicious, so it makes sense to stash it. When he does show, call the cops and let them handle him. You could get hurt if he catches on to you."

Jan thought she detected genuine concern in his voice. Neat.

"Sounds okay to me," she said agreeing. "But if he leaves, I'm following him. Deal?"

He nodded at her. "Deal."

She smiled as she walked to her bike. It was a long shot, but this crazy plan could work.

* * *

Jan had told her mom about going to Banff, but not why. She'd said she was just going for the day to do the tourist thing, which was partly true. Every time she went to the mountain resort, it was like a mini-holiday. However, because she would be going alone, her mom's initial response had been no, it was too dangerous. But after Jan assured her she'd be careful and would be home before it got dark, her mom had given permission.

Getting time off from work on the busiest day of the week was going to be a bigger problem. She didn't want to leave Robin short staffed, but she really needed to be in Banff on Saturday.

It turned out getting the day off was no problem at all. Jan had still not known how to ask her boss when the energetic young woman had come bustling through the back door of the restaurant, instantly infusing the room with her kinetic energy.

"Jan, just the girl I'm looking for," she said cheerily. Jan waited as the slim woman pulled her shoulder length auburn hair into a ponytail and secured it with a bright teal scrunchy that perfectly matched her brightly coloured outfit. "I was wondering about work on Saturday.

What with everything that's been going on, I thought you might like the day off. If you can tear yorself away from here, that is." She winked at her employee and smiled warmly.

Jan grinned at her. "You read my mind. I would love the day off. Thanks Robin. I owe you one." This was going to work out perfectly.

The weather Saturday morning promised to be spectacular for a day in the mountains, warm and sunny with hardly any wind, which made riding a lot more pleasant. Wind gusts could push a little bike like hers all over the road.

She filled up at the gas station and headed west. The day lived up to its advanced billing. Jan smiled as she watched the green pines flash by. The mountains rose all around her, their peaks still brilliant white with lingering snow. The air took on a sharp crispness you only get high in the Rockies.

Her bike ran beautifully. It purred as she held the throttle open and the little machine accelerated effortlessly. She eased off as she approached the park gates. The speed limit was lower in the parks and she didn't want any trouble with police today. She had her park permit stuck to her fairing and pointed to it as she passed the lady in the booth.

Banff was alive with tourists. The streets of the tourist mecca looked wonderful, gaily festooned with flowers everywhere. Planters held bright geraniums in shocking shades of fuchsia and red, while the hanging baskets cascaded candy-striped petunias and trailing lobelia in a dozen different shades. The bright summer sunshine had everyone's spirits up.

Jan parked her bike in the trees just as Josh had suggested. The spot was adjacent to the centre where the bike show was being held and gave her a great view of all the activity. The variety and number of bikes in the parking lot was impressive. *Exactly what a bike thief would be looking for.* She removed her helmet and took up a position under a big pine tree, where she could see not only everyone who entered or left the building, but anyone walking around the parking lot.

She figured the guy would be wearing his helmet so no one could accidentally connect his face with a missing bike. Once she spotted the guy, she'd follow him to his lair and then call David McKenna. Sounded simple enough. Since there were no RCMP swarming the parking lot, she was pretty sure no one had lost a bike yet. She sat down to watch and wait.

The number and variety of bikes coming and going was amazing. Jan vowed to someday own a set of trick leathers like the ones she saw arriving on these high-dollar machines. She scanned the helmets being carried by the visitors. No telltale lightning bolt. The afternoon ticked on and still no sign of her man.

Suddenly she sat up. Coming and going! There were trick bikes all over Banff, not just at the show. This guy was smart. He could take one from anywhere in Banff — a park, a restaurant or the street. If she stayed here she could miss him. When she'd promised Josh she'd stay at the Centre, she hadn't considered the guy's stealing a bike from anywhere but the show. Dumb.

She jumped up and headed back for her bike. There was only one place where she was sure to see this guy — the park gates leading away from Banff. Why hadn't she thought of this sooner? Cursing herself for such a basic slip-up, Jan rode as quickly as possible back to the park gates, praying she hadn't missed him already.

She parked her bike by one of the quaint stone toll-booths that marked the park entrance and exit. It was getting late and the shadows were already creeping across the valley floor. He may already have gone. She mentally kicked herself again. She had probably missed the best chance she had to catch this creep.

An hour later, just as she was about to give up, Jan saw a rider dressed in black leathers approaching quickly on a brand-new red Honda CBR 900RR Fireblade. Her heart skipped a beat as she tried to see his helmet, but he was still too far away. Ducking behind the tollbooth, Jan watched as the rider moved closer. The guy neatly dodged around a car and deftly moved into the far exit lane. He handled the big bike like an expert.

As he closed in on the park gates, she waited for a better look at the rider's helmet. The dark visor obscured his face. Identifying him was impossible. However, there was no mistaking the symbol emblazoned on the side. It was the one she'd been waiting for.

He flashed by and was gone in an instant.

Her fingers shook just a tiny bit as she turned the key and started her bike. It would be hard to catch him, but she had the element of surprise. He didn't know she was coming.

She flattened herself down over the gas tank and opened the throttle up. The little bike jumped as it accelerated. She hoped there were no police with radar hiding as she saw the speedometer edge past the 200-km mark. In the distance she could just make out the rider.

Slowly, slowly she reeled him in. She didn't want to catch him, just get close enough so she wouldn't lose him while he led her to his hideout. The trick was figuring out when she was close enough without being too close.

The light was failing fast now as Jan danced around the cars on the Trans-Canada Highway, which led east to Calgary. If she were right, the guy would split off at the Bragg Creek exit and take her to where he stashed the bikes. This was a different bike than the one she'd seen him on when he'd cut her and her mom off. She was sure he'd stolen this one also.

The road flashed by as she wended her way along the curving mountain highway. She had to slow her speed for the turns, but accelerated out of the corners and down the straights.

When the fast CBR went through a series of bends in the road, Jan worried she'd lose him, and tried to coax a few more Km/hr out of her two-stroke. She came out of the last corner blasting at nearly 160 km per hour. The Honda was nowhere to be seen.

Up ahead were more twists and turns. Maybe the bike was already in the next corner. Jan prayed she hadn't lost the guy. She turned into the next bend hoping to see the taillight of the Honda up ahead.

Nothing. She couldn't understand it. He should have been there.

Suddenly, there was the blinding glare of a headlight in her rearview mirror. The big bike swooped down on her like some giant condor. Jan swerved into the next lane, hoping for some traffic around the next turn to put between her and the menacing bike. There were no cars to use as interference and Jan knew she couldn't outrun the high-powered bike.

It moved up behind her, shadowing her every move. Her knuckles were white as she tried to evade the rider using all her skill. He moved in closer and closer. He was going to force her off the road. Jan looked over the edge of the road and down the steep embankment. She couldn't even see the bottom in the gathering darkness. Taking a slow, deep breath, she concentrated on keeping her bike from flying off into eternity. If she touched the guardrail and went over the edge, she knew she'd never live through the fall.

At this speed, one false move and it would be fatal, even if she did manage to stay on this side of the guardrail. She did the only thing she could think of. Rolling the accelerator back, she applied the brakes as hard as she dared. She hoped the back wheel didn't lock up and put her into a skid. The bike shuddered as it decelerated faster than Jan thought possible. She silently thanked Grey for insisting on those steel-braided brake lines.

The CBR shot past her as her unexpected move caught the driver off guard. If she could stay away from him long enough for some traffic to come along, she'd dodge him using the vehicles as shields. Who'd have thought she'd be wishing for traffic?

The mystery rider must have figured out what she was going to do: she saw his brake light come on ahead of her. She tried to drive around him, but he saw her coming and steered his bike into her path. Jan swerved, hit a patch of gravel on the shoulder and felt her bike lose traction. She tried to recall everything she'd been taught at the race school and managed to pull the bike back under control as she deliberately drove it off the edge of the road.

She and her bike were immediately airborne. She reflexively squeezed the handlebars, which was her big mistake. She should have tried to get away from the bike, instead she landed with the machine — and she landed hard. She remembered smelling gas and hoped nothing was about to catch fire. Then, all she could feel was her leg being pounded into the ground beneath the bike. Pain flashed through her entire body and she could feel herself instantly covered in cold, clammy sweat.

The bike skidded down the hill at the edge of the road, dragging January with it and sending a shower of shale and rocks scattering around her. She came to rest against a large boulder.

Then silence.

Gingerly, she reached up and opened her visor. She could taste the dust in the air around her. Her arm hurt, but she could move it. Her leg, however, was another matter. It was still pinned under the bike. Fortunately, the dirt at the side of the road was fairly loose, so it gave a little.

She tried wiggling her toes. They moved enough to let her know her leg wasn't broken either. It was, however, going to be tricky to lift the bike up enough to pull it free.

Jan started looking around for something to use as a lever to wedge under the bike. Suddenly, several rocks tumbled against her. She looked up toward the highway.

There, standing at the edge of the road above her, was the dark form of the rider who'd forced her off the road. When she saw his black shape silhouetted against the evening sky, her heart seemed to stop beating in her chest. Fear washed over her like an icy wave.

Helplessly, she watched as he started down toward her.

Fighting down panic, Jan futiley pushed on the heavy motorbike. Pain shot through her entire body as she tried to wrench the trapped leg free.

Mesmerized with terror, Jan watched the dark Lightning Rider moving closer.

# Chapter 5

January pushed on the bike with all her strength. She had to free her leg and try to get away. She didn't want to think about what was going to happen when he made it down to her. She felt like a helpless butterfly pinned to a piece of cardboard.

All of a sudden, the ominous helmeted figure stopped, turned and scrambled up the slope.

Jan waited breathlessly. What was he doing? Then she heard his bike start and the back tire squeal as he sped away. She was so relieved; she felt tears starting as she continued to struggle with the bike trapping her leg.

Momentarilly stopping, she became aware of the soft crunch of truck tires coming to a stop on the shoulder. A door opened and the closing strains of a Garth Brooks' country and western tune floated down to her on the cool evening breeze. This was why the guy had left. He'd been scared off.

"Hey, are you okay?" an old man in a faded Calgary Flames ball cap called down to her.

She began frantically trying to dig the dirt out from under her leg to free it. Jan gritted her teeth and gave a hard pull on her leg. She felt her leg move out from under the bike.

Slowly, she started to get to her feet. "I think I'm okay. I need a phone so I can call …" She was just about to say the police, but realized she couldn't. What would she tell them? Who would believe her without proof? The Banff RCMP would call the Bragg Creek Police and then Gellar would be involved. She'd lost enough credibility.

"So I can call a tow truck to pull my bike up out of this ditch," she finished lamely as she gingerly stood up on her twisted leg.

"No need," he said, grinning at her. "I just got a brand-new Warn winch I've been dying to try out on somebody. You just hold on and I'll be down in a minute."

Jan's leg felt stiff and sore, but it held her weight. So far so good, she thought, relieved, then she tugged her helmet off and looked down at her bike.

Grey would freak when he saw how she'd bent the little 350. She rubbed her shoulder. She was going to be awfully sore tomorrow.

"Hey, mister," she asked, wincing as she wiggled her toes in her boot. "Did you see another bike leaving as you pulled up?"

The man looked puzzled. "I'm not sure. Maybe it was a bike that was going around the corner up ahead, couldn't swear to it. I didn't really get a good look. You riding with a friend, were you, young lady?"

"No, I wouldn't call him my friend. You could say I was alone." She sighed, so much for corroboration of her story.

The next half-hour was spent pulling, dragging and hoisting her bike out of the ravine. The winch on the 4x4 really got a workout.

When the bike was finally sitting on the side of the road, Jan gave a sigh of relief. Maybe it wasn't that bad after all, she thought, as she straightened the license plate.

"You're not planning on riding this thing home, are you, miss? If you like I can give you a ride back to Banff and you can call your folks," the Good Samaritan offered as he lifted his old hat and scratched the bald spot on the top of his head.

"No, I don't need to call my mom." That was the last thing she wanted to do. "But thanks so much for all your help. If I can get it started, I think it will make it home. Besides, from here it will take as long for us to go back to Banff, as it will for me to make it home." Jan swung her leg over the seat.

Her leg screamed as she kicked the starter over.

The motor tried to catch, but couldn't quite make it. From the smell, Jan knew what was the matter. The bike was flooded and would have to dry out for a while. She climbed off and began a quick inspection to see what had made it through the crash and what hadn't. By the time she'd walked around the bike and looked at the broken mirror, dented tank and busted signal lights, she knew it was going to be expensive. So much for buying a new set of leathers with her saved tip money.

She sighed and tried the bike again. It coughed, sputtered, but finally, to her relief, the noisy little two-stroke caught. She feathered the throttle until the engine cleared and would hold an idle by itself. It sounded okay.

"I've got to go all the way to Bragg Creek. Would you mind following me for a little way, just until I'm sure it will run?" she asked the old gentleman.

"No problem, miss. I'm heading back to Calgary anyway. You just take your time and I'll follow you all the way to the Bragg Creek turnoff." He smiled at her. "You sure you're okay to ride?"

Jan pulled her helmet back on and tightened the strap. "I'll be fine. Thanks again for all your help." She smiled and shook his hand. "You'll never know how much I owe you."

Boy, that was sure the truth, she thought as she climbed slowly onto her bike. Now the adrenaline rush had worn off, her muscles were starting to tighten up. She tapped it into first gear and slowly accelerated, hoping the bruised bike wouldn't fail.

The ride home seemed to take forever. When she finally pulled into her driveway, all she could think about was sinking into a hot bath and crawling into bed for about two days. Jan carefully tucked her bike around the side of the garage where her mom wouldn't see it and start asking questions.

* * *

Josh was waiting for her when she got to work the next day.

"What happened to you yesterday?" he asked. "When I didn't hear from you, I got worried. Did you find the guy?"

"I found him all right, then he found me." She briefly told him what had happened. Josh just stared at her, becoming more and more agitated as she related the details. "And next time, I'll be ready for him," she concluded. "He'll be the one who ends up in the dust."

"Are you crazy? I told you what could happen with a maniac like this. I said to wait at the Centre. But no, you had to go off on your own and nearly got yourself killed. You should stop trying to catch this guy yourself, Jan. It's getting out of control." He was practically shouting at her.

She was so surprised she couldn't speak.

There was a break in the tirade as he stopped to take a puff on his inhaler. Then he sighed, shaking his head. "Look, I'm sorry, Jan. It's just I was ... worried about you." He ran his hand through his hair. "Are you sure you're okay. Maybe you should see a doctor." He sounded so concerned, Jan tried to reassure him.

"No, I'm fine, really, just a few bruises, a couple of bumps and a little road rash. It's my bike that's really broken up." She rubbed her aching back. "Let me give you a little piece of advice, Josh. If you ever decide to crash Ol' Lucifer, don't land with the bike, get as far away from the machine as you can. It will save you being pounded into the ground." She grinned up at him. "Speaking of crashing my bike, Grey's going to have a fit when I tell him the guys at the garage had to do some work on it. He doesn't like anyone messing with that bike but him. However, if I'm going to be street legal, I have to have little things like working signal lights or Constable McKenna will be writing me out a ticket or two."

"What about going to the police? Did you report the guy?" he asked.

"Right, the Métis girl is up to her old tricks again," Jan scoffed. "No witnesses, no proof, Gellar would laugh me out of the station. Nope, I'll get this guy on my own."

She worked a little slower than she usually did and by the time her shift was over, her aching muscles and bruised body reminded her she hadn't come through the accident completely unscathed.

When she pulled into her driveway, there was a police car parked where she usually left her bike. Probably David. He was around quite a bit lately, on duty and off.

She manoeuvred her bike between her mom's car and the police cruiser by duck walking it, and stopped up by the garage door. The garage was a small freestanding building next to the house. Her mom said she was glad it was separate when Grey and Jan were working on their bikes. Revving engines at two o'clock in the morning was not her idea of a fun hobby.

Jan went in through the enclosed porch at the back of the house. In the old days it would probably have been called a mudroom, someplace you kicked off your boots before entering the house. She took off her coat and hung it up. Her shoulders throbbed and her leg ached. She was glad to be home.

Their house was made of logs and was not what anyone would call large. It was more what you'd call a rustic cabin, with the garage the only concession to modern architecture.

Jan stepped into the kitchen just as her mom came through the living room door.

"Sergeant Gellar's here, January," she began, skipping her usual greeting. "Apparently, there were other bikes stolen prior to the one Grey crashed on. He's saying Grey is involved in all the thefts and wants to question him. I told him Grey is in a coma, but he insists on talking to him as soon as he regains consciousness."

Her face looked strained. "I tried to tell him Grey had nothing to do with those thefts, but his mind seems made up." She took a deep breath and smoothed a wisp of hair that had escaped from her braid. Jan noticed for the first time that there was a thread of grey among the glossy black strands.

"I know he's only doing his job, but to tell the truth Jan, the man's a little annoying." She smiled tiredly at her daughter. "I'm glad you're home. Shall we go talk to the lion, Daniel?"

Jan sighed. This was not what she wanted to come home to but there was no way she could get out of it. She smiled back at her mom and followed her into the living room. She really was too exhausted to deal with Sergeant Gellar right now, but she knew her mom expected it.

The sergeant was silhouetted against the curtains when Jan came into the living room.

"Hello, Miss Fournier." His face looked grim. "I noticed you pull up. From the new dents and scratches I saw on your bike, it looks like you've had a spill. Did you recently have an accident?"

He had a way of messing things up without even trying, Jan thought as she saw her mother's face react.

"Jan, is this true? Did you have an accident on your bike?" Her mom suddenly looked even more strained.

"Nothing serious, Mom," she said, trying to make light of the incident.

"Care to tell us what happened?" Gellar asked in a tone Jan didn't trust.

"Actually, it was on Saturday when I was coming back from Banff." She would have liked to lie to Gellar just to get him off her back, but she just couldn't bring herself to do it, especially in front of her mom.

She sighed, maybe she should tell the sergeant about the mystery biker. It wasn't like he was going to believe her and issue an APB on the Lightning Rider, though.

She took a deep breath. "I was following this guy who had the same helmet on as the one who ran us off the road. You remember, Mom, the one with the lightning bolt motif down the sides. I think he's involved in the bike thefts, the ones Grey's falsely accused of," she added pointedly. "I had a good idea this guy would be at the big bike show in Banff this weekend and I knew he wouldn't be able to resist stealing a bike. I waited at the park gates so I could follow him to his hideout when he came through, but instead he followed me and forced me off the road. I'm okay, but the bike got a little bent."

She hoped that was explanation enough because she suddenly felt really tired.

Her mom just stared at her, confusion on her face.

"Were there any witnesses to this assault?" Sergeant Gellar asked.

"Actually ... no," Jan said weakly, knowing how that sounded.

"Let me get this straight. You were run off the Trans-Canada Highway in broad daylight on a Saturday afternoon and no one saw the incident?" Gellar's tone was one Jan was getting used to hearing.

"I know it sounds strange, for some reason, the timing between vehicles on the highway was weird. There was no traffic on that stretch of the road for the time it took for the guy to run me into the ground. However, there was a gentleman who came along right after and helped me with my bike. He thought he might have seen a bike taillight disappearing ahead of me," Jan said defensively.

"He *thought* he *might* have seen a taillight? Did you get this expert witness's name?" Gellar asked.

"Ah, actually, no I didn't." Jan was mentally kicking herself, but she'd been so shaken up at the time, she hadn't thought of it.

"Are you sure you didn't just lose control of your bike and made up this mystery biker to add credibility to your story? Perhaps you'd been illegally drinking in Banff and didn't want your mother to know. Is that why you didn't notify the police when you had the accident, Miss Fournier?"

Jan was angry at the turn the conversation had taken. "Of course I wasn't drinking," she said a little too loudly. "There *was* a guy on a bike. He ran me off the road." She clenched her fists as she tried to regain control.

"I think that's enough, Sergeant Gellar." Her mother's quiet voice cut through the escalating interrogation, asserting a calm control.

Gellar stopped his tirade.

"If my daughter says there was another bike that forced her off the road, there *was* another bike. My daughter doesn't lie." Her mom hadn't raised her voice, but Jan knew Gellar had somehow backed down.

His hard, grey eyes narrowed as he continued to stare at Jan. "It's a serious offence to file a false report, especially an uncorroborated one in which you are obviously trying to shift the blame for the bike thefts from your brother by trying to introduce a phoney new suspect." He pulled the front of his tunic down and straightened his posture. "I hope I've made myself clear."

He turned to her mom. "If you happen to remember anything more about Grey's activities that might help with the investigation, please contact me at the police station. Good day, Mrs. Fournier." He nodded curtly to her mom and strode to the front door. Jan and her mom just stood rooted to the spot until he left.

"Maybe you'd better tell me everything that's been going on, young lady," her mom said the second the door closed behind Sergeant Gellar.

Jan knew she'd better come clean. She explained everything, including her theory about the biker and the thefts. Her mom sat quietly and listened. When Jan had finished, she nodded slowly.

"I'm going to make a cup of tea. Do you want one?" she asked.

Jan shook her head slowly, caught off guard by her mom's reaction or lack of reaction to the story. She knew her mom was going to give the whole situation a lot of thought before she decided anything. It was a good sign she hadn't immediately forbidden Jan from any further investigation on her own.

Maybe she'd have Grey cleared before her mom came to any decision. "No thanks to the tea, Mom. I'm going to go have a long, hot soak."

"Okay, honey, and January, don't worry about Sergeant Gellar. I've dealt with his type before. We can handle him. You go have your bath." She smiled at Jan as though nothing out of the ordinary had just been discussed. "Oh, I forgot to tell you. I got a call from your cousin Samuel. Both Samuel and Doug will be riding in the rodeo this weekend. He wanted to make sure we'd be there to cheer the family on."

"The Tsuu T'ina Powwow is this coming weekend? I guess it slipped my mind." She swallowed a lump in her throat. "Grey loves the rodeo. He'll be sorry when he finds out he missed it." She smiled weakly at her mom and headed upstairs.

With everything that had been going on, Jan had completely forgotten about the rodeo that would take place next weekend. The annual summer event had always been a high point for Jan and Grey. It was when they got together with family and First Nations friends from all over Canada and the United States who spent the summer on the Powwow trail.

It was a favourite holiday for a lot of families and if they had relatives competing in either the rodeo events or the traditional dancing contests, there was the possibility of making some real money.

Each powwow had purses for the rodeo events as well as the Native dancing and drumming, some in the thousands of dollars. The Tsuu T'ina Powwow was a big one with hundreds of families attending.

When Jan had been younger, one of her cousins had tried to teach her how to Fancy Dance. Jan didn't have the patience or coordination to learn the steps to the complicated dance that was performed with an elaborate costume, including a beautiful shawl designed to sway gracefully as she moved. Neither Jan nor the shawl, however, had swayed with anything even remotely like grace. She'd given it up after one summer. A girl had to know her limits.

Bragg Creek was a friendly town and everyone looked forward to the powwow, everyone except Sergeant Gellar, Jan thought bitterly. He always made sure there were extra officers on duty. It was his way of letting the people at the powwow know that he was watching them — closely, waiting for one of the Indians to make a mistake. The fact the Tsuu T'ina celebration was a dry event, no liquor allowed, didn't matter to Gellar. How one man could be so ignorant was a mystery to Jan.

Remembering the powwow made Jan think of her Aunt Rose from Brocket and her famous homemade Saskatoon jam. Every year, she and Grey would pig out on fresh, fried bannock slathered in her aunt's jam.

It would be strange going without her brother and Jan wondered if she would enjoy it as much.

Jan looked forward to seeing her cousins, the Big Bears. She knew they would bring their traditional teepee and set it up on the grounds. The teepee turned into a focal point for friends to visit and because the dancing continued all night long, people would drop in at any and all hours. The celebration lasted the entire weekend.

Grey would be sad he missed out, Jan thought as she ran a steaming hot bath. Her muscles ached and she felt extremely tired. The idea of going to the rodeo and enjoying herself made her feel guilty when she thought of her brother lying in that white hospital bed.

She promised herself she'd make it up to Grey next year. Smiling, Jan decided she'd let her brother eat all the fresh bannock and jam or hang around the corrals and discuss the horses, which was another of Grey's favourite activities. Anything he wanted.

Feeling a little better, Jan started to think about the weekend and suddenly wondered if Josh would like to go with her to watch the events. That would be nice.

She settled back into the hot, soothing water. While Jan was soaking, she heard her mom on the phone. Her voice was low and she talked for a long time. Jan couldn't make out the words, but she had a good idea who her mom was talking to.

\* \* \*

The next morning, Jan was just getting off her bike when she spotted Josh swiftly crossing the parking lot of the mall where they worked.

"Hey, Josh," she called as she waved. He slowed down while Jan ran to catch up.

"Where's the fire?" she asked as she fell into step beside him.

"No fire, I just have a lot of stuff to do this morning." He continued toward the post office.

"It's the Tsuu T'ina Powwow this weekend and I was wondering … If you weren't busy, maybe you'd like to go with me. My cousins are riding in the rodeo and —"

He interrupted her. "I'm going to be busy."

"But you don't even know when I'm going," she said, trying not to show how bruised her feelings were.

"Look, I meant to say I'm going to be busy all weekend. I've got something really important to do." Then he noticed her disappointment. "Hey, I'm sorry. Besides, I think you'll really like my surprise."

What could she say? "Sure, Josh, it's okay." She changed the subject. "What surprise?" she asked, wondering what he was up to.

"If I told you, it wouldn't be a surprise would it? See you later," he said as he pulled the door open and went in before Jan could say anything.

Jan turned back toward her bike. She wondered if the surprise involved her. She smiled to herself. That would be nice, too.

* * *

David McKenna was now driving them into Calgary pretty regularly to visit Grey. Jan liked the way he could make her mom laugh. In fact, David was a one-man support group.

They were just walking down the hall toward the nurses' desk, when Dr. Singh saw them. He grinned and strode over.

"I'm glad you're here. I was just going to call you. We have good news," he said, walking with them toward Grey's room.

"What news? What is it, Doctor?" her mom asked.

"It seems someone dropped off a special gift for Grey. A special swatch of grass, which had been braided and, the nurse tells me, blessed," he said, smiling.

"Yes, it was sweetgrass sent by Grey's great-uncle," her mother said, unsure where this conversation was going.

"Well, it seems our boy liked the gift so much, he decided to wake up and see it for himself." The doctor nodded. "He came out of his coma about an hour ago and the first thing he did was to reach for that grass on his bedside table."

Jan squeezed her mom's hand and felt the rosary in her palm.

"Can we see him, Doctor?" Jan asked.

"I think that would be a good idea. However, he is still a little fuzzy, not quite himself. It may be awhile before he's fully cognitive," he said with some reservation. "This is entirely normal."

David, Jan and her mom entered Grey's room. He looked so different without the ventilator. He still had a small cannula at his nose supplying extra oxygen, but compared to the horrible plastic hose and machinery associated with a ventilator, this was nothing.

Jan watched her brother breathing — he was doing it himself, slowly and regularly, which made her feel ridiculously happy.

His face still looked tired, but now it was a good tired, like he'd won some sort of battle. His dark skin looked a little off-colour and the hollows in his cheeks seemed deeper than Jan remembered. The nurses had washed and braided his long, black hair and Jan thought her brother looked the best she'd ever seen him. She smiled at the pink ribbons the nurses had used to secure the bottom of the braids. Grey obviously hadn't seen this little detail because, sick or not, he wouldn't have put up with them.

Jan noticed, almost as an afterthought, most of the intravenous lines were gone also. It was funny how soon you could get used to something.

Together, Jan and her mom walked up to his bed.

"Grey, it's me," her mom said quietly.

Grey opened his eyes and turned his head toward her.

"Hello, sweatheart," she said, smiling down at him.

He looked at her. "Hi, Mom," he said in a weak voice, his lips curving in a barely perceptible smile.

Jan took his hand. "Hi, big brother. Welcome back." She smiled at him.

"Jan, you're here." It seemed to be a great effort, but he smiled at her. "I've got a splitting headache."

They laughed and Jan saw her mom's eyes were bright with tears.

"Yeah, well you earned it," Jan said, grinning.

"Thanks for the sweetgrass," he said, eyeing the braid on his table. "It was the oddest thing. I dreamed I was lying in a field and the sun was shining. All around me I could smell the warm, summer grass. It was great. I just laid there with my eyes closed enjoying the sun and the sweet smell of the grass." He took a deep breath. "Then, somehow, I knew it was a dream and it was time to wake up." He closed his eyes as though just talking had worn him out.

"You should thank the constable," her mom said, smiling warmly at David. "He went to some trouble to get it for you."

Grey looked over to the door where David had been quietly standing. "Thanks, David." He glanced at his mom out of the corner of his eye, then back at David. "I mean Constable?"

Jan giggled and her mom tried to hide her smile.

David grinned at Grey. "You're welcome, Grey."

"Something else in my dream." He looked puzzled. "I had a dog with me, a big white dog. It was the oddest thing."

Jan looked over at her mom. "We'll have to have a family discussion about this once Grey's feeling better." Her mom just nodded.

They visited for a short while, then when Grey started getting tired, they decided it was time to go.

"I just have one more question, Grey," Jan began. Their visit had gone so well, she wasn't sure she should ask about the bike, but she had to know.

She leaned toward him and spoke very clearly and slowly. "Grey, about your accident, the bike you were on when you crashed was stolen. I need to know who gave you the Bimota." She looked into her brother's bruised face, searching his eyes. "I have to know, Grey."

He shook his head, and then a frown creased his face. "Jan I can't remember anything about that day. It's a total blank."

Jan just stared at him. She couldn't believe what she was hearing. "What do you mean you don't remember?" she questioned. "You remember me and Mom. Why can't you remember where that bike came from?" She didn't understand.

He shook his head weakly. "I don't remember even being on a bike. I don't know where it came from or who gave it to me." He saw the look on her face. "I'm sorry, Jan, but I can't help you."

Jan could see he was too tired to talk anymore. She walked from the room, confused. How could he not remember something as important as this?

"Jan, don't be discouraged," her mom said, putting her arm around Jan as they walked down the hallway. "The doctor said he'd be fuzzy for a while. He just needs to rest a little longer, then I'm sure everything will be straightened out."

David agreed with her mom. "It's often the case with head injuries as severe as Grey's."

Jan nodded. "Sure, you're right." But she couldn't help thinking it was very strange.

* * *

Jan and her mom had arrived at the Tsuu T'ina Pow-wow grounds early on Saturday. They'd gone first to visit Jan's aunt and had spent some time catching up on news and enjoying tea and fresh bannock. Her aunt had been upset to hear about Grey and would personally take him a jar of her Saskatoon jam.

Later, once all the visiting had been done with friends and family, Jan and her mom wandered around the various booths, checking out all the different merchandise offered.

There were First Nations merchants from all over the United States and Canada, with a wide variety of items for sale. There were blankets from New Mexico, at a very good price, and bead strings for putting that finishing touch on dancing costumes. One booth had lots of different clothes and intricately beaded moccasins, which Jan and her mom admired. Everywhere there was a carnival atmosphere with kids laughing and running while adults got caught up on a year's worth of news.

Jan had bought a beautiful silver feather brooch, which a Navajo vendor had for sale. It was intricately detailed and Jan had loved it. It hadn't been hard to bargain the price down to a manageable level, especially when her mom had said she'd take another just like it. They'd both loved the look of the delicate metal sculpture.

The Saturday crowd was animated and noisy as Jan and her mom climbed to the top of the bleachers for the afternoon's rodeo events. It was a beautiful afternoon. The sun was wonderfully warm — even hot, which, because of the altitude, was unusual for the Creek and that never-ending blue Alberta sky didn't have a cloud in it. Perfect rodeo weather.

Their seats were high enough that they caught whatever breeze wafted their way. This turned out to be a nice bonus as the afternoon wore on and the temperatures continued to climb.

"Your cousin's up next," her mom said and Jan turned to the chutes at the far end of the arena. It was the calf-roping event and Jan knew it wasn't as easy as it looked at the Calgary Stampede.

Everyone waited expectantly as the calf was loaded into the stall and the cowboy and his horse prepared for the race. Jan could see her cousin Doug winding his rope so it was exactly the right length for throwing. He seemed to sit taller in the saddle this year than he had last. The other cowboys had all had great times and Doug was going to have to snag that calf right out of the chute to beat them.

With a nod of his head, her cousin signalled to the man at the gate that he was ready. Suddenly, the sturdy wooden gate was thrown open and the calf started running for the far end of the infield. Doug was instantly after the young steer, his big horse exploding out of the chute.

Holding it with one hand, he swung his lariat above him as they charged after the calf. Then, at just the exact moment, he sent it sailing over the animal's head. The bawling calf ran straight into the loop on the rope, which tightened as Doug's horse braced itself against the steer's headlong flight. Before the horse had completely stopped, Doug was off and running with the pigging string he'd use to lash the calf's hooves together — if he could get the animal wrestled to the ground.

The crowd was yelling and whistling because they knew a large calf like Doug's was going to be trouble. Jan watched breathlessly, then started cheering as her cousin wrestled the struggling animal, flipped it over and tied its legs together in a lightning move that had everyone on their feet cheering.

It was a thing of beauty to behold, for calf-roping cowboys and fans alike. She stuck her fingers in her mouth and started whistling loudly. Her mom was clapping enthusiastically.

Doug won the calf roping, but her cousin Samuel was thrown from his horse during the bronc riding and didn't score. He'd limped over to the fence grinning from ear to ear and Jan could see he was okay with his defeat. Besides, there was another day of competition before the finals.

The sun was starting to sink lower in the western sky and was now directly in Jan's eyes. She held her hand up and tried to block her face from the glare.

"Mom, I forgot my shades, and since you have your chapeau with you," Jan said, smiling at her mom, who was wearing a large sun hat, "do you think I could borrow yours?"

Her mom just shook her head. "January, you really should be better organized." She rummaged in her purse and extricated the sunglasses. Jan slipped them on.

The dark polarizing glasses allowed her to see the entire infield clearly, in fact, she thought as she glanced around, she could see right to the highway that ran past the rodeo grounds.

A sudden movement on the road caught her eye. She stared, watching the object get closer.

It was a big, powerful bike, exactly the same as the one that had run her off the road last weekend. Her heart began to beat faster. A red, CBR 900RR wasn't that exotic, true, but the additional fact the rider was in black leathers made her sure she had to check it out.

"I'll meet you at Aunt Rose's later, Mom," she called as she grabbed her leather jacket and began running down the stairs of the wooden bleachers.

Her mom started to say something, but Jan was moving too fast to hear.

There was no time to think about what she was doing if she were going to follow this guy. If she stopped to call the police, he's be long gone and so would her opportunity to perhaps find out who the real thief was.

She was really glad she'd decided to ride her bike, which meant she had access to her own wheels. She wriggled into her jacket as she ran.

Scrambling to her bike, she had her key out and in the ignition in a second. Her helmet was on and buckled as she kicked the bike over and slammed it into gear. The back tire spun, sending dirt and debris flying, as she sped after the big Honda.

The road through the parking area was one-way, but if she followed it, she'd have to go all around the outside of the grounds to get to the exit. Ignoring the parking people and their red flags, she shot down the *in* road and past the stream of traffic coming toward her. She could hear the yelling over the chatter of her bike engine as she sped out onto the highway.

She raced after the bike hoping the rider wouldn't spook if he saw her coming up on him in his mirrors.

This could be her chance to catch the bike thief and clear Grey once and for all.

Up ahead she saw a brake light come on as the big bike turned off the main road and headed into Bragg Creek. Jan leaned into the corner, then pulled the bike upright and began braking.

She followed him through town and into the secluded Mountain Pines Park where he stopped the big bike. If this was the guy, the park was not the best place to confront him. It was tucked away in a grove of trees and was usually deserted. However, she had no choice. She would do anything to help her brother. Jan pulled in behind him and shut down her engine.

Jumping off her bike, she ran to grab the rider, who was just dismounting.

Spinning the guy around, Jan's heart was pounding in her chest as she looked up at the black-helmeted rider. "You!" she said, staring at the face behind the visor.

# Chapter 6

"January, what do you think you're doing?" Josh asked angrily as he flipped open his visor.

"Josh, what are *you* doing on *this* bike?" she asked, ignoring his question and overriding it with her own.

"I'm trying to take it home, but some nutcase chased me so hard, I thought I'd better stop and see what she wanted." His anger seemed to evaporate as he turned to the bike. Patting the shining new machine, he smiled. "Well, what do you think? Pretty nice, huh? I just picked her up in Calgary."

Jan's mind was whirling. It was then she noticed his helmet. It was a new black Shoei, an expensive one, but it didn't have a lightning bolt.

She refocused on Josh. "What do you mean you just picked it up? You never told me you were buying a new bike. It must have cost a fortune and why did you get such a big bike? You'll kill yourself on this thing …" She trailed off, realizing how she must sound. She just hadn't expected the rider to be Josh.

"What is this, the Spanish Inquisition? I told you I had a surprise," he said defensively.

She backpeddled, trying to smooth things out. "I ... I'm sorry. It's just that the guy who rode me off the road last week was on the same kind of bike and he had on black leathers too." She deflated. "I didn't see your helmet was different or I would have known."

"Jan, lots of people have black leathers — it's probably the most common colour going. You know that, besides, I got a great deal on the helmet when I bought the leathers. I couldn't pass up the bargain." He grinned at her. She nodded, agreeing, then glancing over his new outfit, noticed how great he looked in it.

"No offence, Josh, but why did you get such a big bike? It's not like you've ever ridden something this powerful before."

"After our conversation the other night about new bikes, I decided the time had come for me to trade in Ol' Lucifer. I had some money from the calves I sold this spring and decided to get something I wouldn't outgrow too quickly. It took a bit of convincing, but finally, my parents said it was my money. And I think I deserve this bike." He held up a hand to stop her protest. "I know it's too big for me now, but just because it will go mach 4, doesn't mean I have to drive it at mach 4."

She could see the logic of his argument. It *was* a beautiful machine. She looked at the sleek lines and state-of-the-art everything. It would be awhile before Canadian champion road racer Miguel Duhamel outgrew this bike.

Jan smiled at him. "It is a wicked ride. I'll have to get Grey to tune my little rocket up the minute he gets out just so I can stay in your mirrors." The thought of Grey brought a mental flash of him lying in the hospital. It made her throat feel tight as she swallowed back the worry. What if he never regained his memory about the

85

bike? It was going to be pretty tough proving Grey's innocence when he couldn't defend himself.

She changed the subject. "I was just at the powwow with my mom. She's going to wonder where I went in such a hurry. I'd better get back before she sends out the cavalry." The reference to cavalry at an Indian event made her giggle. "We can go for a ride later if you want. You'd get a feel for the bike and I'd get a great ride in."

"Sounds good. I'll meet you at the junction to Highway 66 at seven o'clock and we can head up into the mountains." He slid the visor closed on the aerodynamic helmet.

"You're on," she said, smiling. As she drove back to the powwow, she thought about meeting Josh later. It made her feel good.

Her mom was at her Aunt's teepee having a cup of tea when Jan got back. She made a lame excuse about having seen a friend and then escaped to go watch the dancing. Now was no time to explain everything about Josh and the mistaken identity. Besides, it was just about time for Grand Entry, when all the dancers in their beautiful beaded and feathered costumes would enter the dance pavilion in a procession headed by the elders. At a gathering as large as the Tsuu T'ina celebration, there were a lot of dancers in every class. The prize money was substantial and the competition fierce. It was fun to watch and pick your favourite dancer, then see if the judges agreed with you.

As Jan entered the crowded dance pavilion, she spotted some of her cousins sitting in the bleachers waiting. She manoeuvred through the crowd to sit with them. They'd be able to point out more of the finer points of the dancing, which added to the enjoyment.

As she watched the procession of dancers, Jan kept an eye on her watch. She didn't want to be late for her ride with Josh. She smiled to herself. He had looked especially good in his new leathers.

* * *

The Sunday morning breakfast crowd was heavier than usual at the restaurant as tourists out from Calgary for a day in the country took advantage of Robin's varied and exotic menu. The powwow added to the traffic, along with the usual farmers' market crowd and hikers and bikers.

By eleven o'clock, there wasn't a parking space left in the lot. Residents knew weekends were for tourists and tried to accommodate the crowds of visitors who descended on the tiny hamlet.

The restaurants were always the busiest. Jan smiled at Robin as she chatted with some folks over from Dublin on a holiday. Jan heard her telling them about a local cowboy singer who'd put a Celtic twist on old classics for a new sound.

She pushed through the swinging doors to the kitchen.

Jan had told Josh about Grey's amnesia when they'd gone for their ride. He thought it strange that Grey couldn't remember anything about the bike, but could remember everything else.

Jan watched Josh prepare an appetizer. "That was a great ride last night. We'll have to try it again when you get a little more experience on that new machine of yours."

Josh nodded in agreement, but didn't say anything as he deftly arranged an order of samosas on a small plate.

"You did great considering the huge difference between this bike and your old one," Jan went on. "You've got a lot more horsepower now than you had with Ol'

Lucifer." Josh hadn't been the most expert of riders on the new bike. In fact, there were times when Jan had deliberately slowed down or chosen an easier road because she didn't think Josh was up to it. He'd done the smart thing and hadn't pushed the powerful machine anywhere near its capabilities.

Jan thought this was a good strategy. Accidents due to overconfidence were the biggest problem with riders who went up to these big machines too quickly. She knew Josh could ride. He handled Ol' Lucifer well. If he just took his time getting used to the new bike, everything would work out fine.

The afternoon was just as busy as breakfast. Robin, who'd been thrilled at the news of Grey's progress, left for a short errand once the lunch rush was over, but said she'd be back later. About four o'clock, Collin and his entourage surged into the restaurant like an out of control flash flood.

Jan sighed, knowing she wouldn't be able to cash out as early as she'd hoped.

Grabbing a handful of menus, she headed to the new table.

"Can I get you anything to drink while you decide what you'd like to order?" she asked in her best professional tone.

Collin was the only one who'd opened his menu. The others were obviously waiting for him to order for all of them. Jan gave Collin a short second to say something, then smiled. "I'll just give you a minute to decide, shall I?" She moved to clear a table that had just left.

Collin watched her collect all the dishes from the table and when her arms were full, he waved the menu at her.

"I think we're ready to order now, Miss Fournier." He grinned at her like he'd done something really clever.

"I'll be right back, Collin," she said, heading for the kitchen and ignoring his menu waving.

"Sometimes Collin can be such a jerk," she said, dumping the dishes beside the sink.

"Hey, I'm not arguing with you," Josh said, checking the soup pot. "If they order the soup du jour, tell them we're all out." He pulled the big soup pot out of the warming tray.

Jan giggled. "It's Collin and company. If I were you, I'd fire up the pizza oven." She headed back out to take their order.

As she approached the table she heard the group laughing.

"You're definitely in a different tax bracket than I am, Collin. You just got your Camaro four months ago and that's a high-dollar set of fast wheels. Now these novelties." It was Zero Chung, one of Collin's friends, teasing. "Why, that new jacket of yours must have set you back six bills and I wouldn't even guess how much that camera cost."

It was then Jan noticed the expensive leather jacket hanging on the back of Collin's chair and the fancy motor-drive camera sitting on the table. The group was passing around pictures which, Jan guessed, had been taken with the new camera.

"Making the money's no problem, Zero, old bud," Colin said expansively, leaning back in his chair until the front legs were off the floor. "It's finding bigger and better ways to spend it that takes real genius." The whole table laughed.

"I thought you said you blew the bank when you got the new CD sound system for your car, but I guess there was more where that came from." Zero grinned, shaking his head, as he shuffled through a pack of pictures.

Jan stood listening.

"Hey, Jan, come look at these cool pictures Collin took with his new camera," Zero said, holding out a handful of glossy prints. "They look like something out of *National Geographic*. Really professional, here have a look."

Jan leafed through the bright pictures. "These are good. Collin, I didn't know you were a photographer."

She could see Collin puff up almost visibly as he basked in the spotlight.

"Just one of my many talents." He held up one of the pictures for her to see. "Keep in mind this is off the first roll, and I was still getting used to all the bells and whistles, but there are some great shots. This one is of Elbow Falls. Notice the way I caught the rainbow effect from the spray of the water. And this one." He held up another. "I used a macro lens to get the detail in this moss."

"How about this one. I've never seen one like it. How'd you do it?" Zero asked as he scrutinized a multi-image picture.

"I put some of my artsy filters to work and voilà, it repeated the image in this star pattern." Collin was on a roll now as he tutored the uninitiated.

Jan looked more closely at the picture. There were many images of the same subject on the print. It was a shot of a stone cairn that was familiar, but she couldn't place it. In the background, partially hidden by a copse of trees, was an old line shack.

"Where was this shot taken, Collin?" she asked, frowning, unable to place the site.

Collin hesitated. "Oh that's some marker I spotted just north of Cochrane. Now this one ..." He picked another picture off the table, then stopped. "Hey, Jan, I almost forgot. Could we get a couple of extra-large Bragg Specials with orange pop all around?"

"Ah, yeah, sure," she said, heading for the kitchen. There was something about that picture taken by Cochrane that was familiar.

"So what does the King of Cool and his Band of Dreary Men want this time?" Josh asked as she came into the kitchen.

"Oh ... just the usual — two extra-large Bragg Specials with orange pops. He's got a new toy, a fancy camera, and he's holding a photography seminar." She made a face at Josh and started filling the pop order.

As Jan finished filling the pitcher of pop. Robin came through the back door, carrying a box loaded with supplies for the restaurant. She set the box down next to the sink.

Jan glanced at the clock. Yes! 5:01 and her shift was over.

"I hear our little friend is in again," Robin said as the noise from Collin's table spilled into the kitchen.

Jan smiled and explained the reason for the gathering as Robin checked her till float in preparation for starting her shift.

"I don't know where that boy gets his cash from," she said, shaking her head. "It's sure not his dad. Ever since the crash with the motorbike when Collin was so drunk, I know Ed Watson's made that boy pay his own way for extras. Collin must have a fairy godfather with deep pockets."

"I just wish some of that gold dust would land on me," Jan said, finishing her cash-out. "I've got a bike that could use a few dollars in repairs."

Jan filled Robin in on any details she might need to know, then grabbed her gear and headed for the parking lot.

She felt a twinge as she walked toward her battered bike. The paint was scratched and her gas tank dented from the accident. Grey was going to give her hell.

It was too nice a day to go straight home, she decided as she turned her bike toward the mountains.

Highway 66 was a gateway to the Kananaskis and Jan knew that's exactly where she was going to go. As the road sped beneath her two wheels, she started to relax, letting go of the day's pressures and enjoying the ride.

The scenery was inspiring and, as the elevation became higher, she could feel her spirit climb along with the bike. She passed all the familiar landmarks as she continued west into the mountains.

With a jolt, it hit her. Collin's picture! It hadn't been taken near Cochrane. It was a picture of John Ware's Cairn. The stone marker was at the homestead site of the first black rancher in Alberta. It was located near Highway 66, on a remote side road, not far from where she was now.

He couldn't have been that far out on his directions. Collin grew up around here and even though most people didn't know where the cairn was, if he'd taken a picture of it with his new camera, he'd been there recently.

Jan thought about this. It didn't make sense. Did Collin misdirect her on purpose? But why? Why did it matter if someone knew where the picture was really taken? What was he hiding? She remembered what Robin had said about money. Where had Collin managed to get all his newfound wealth he'd been flashing around? Robin had been sure it wasn't from his dad and everyone knew Collin didn't have a job. He was one of the few kids around who didn't have to work and wasn't shy about reminding his buddies of the fact.

Then how was he coming up with such large amounts of cash that he could buy a new car, fancy CD system, leather jacket and camera? Maybe he was winning big at his dad's poker nights. But he only sat in when one of the regulars was away and, from the pizza orders, that wasn't very often.

Something about the poker pizzas made her frown. What was it? Suddenly, she knew.

She jammed on the brakes and turned into one of the many spectacular viewpoints that lined the mountain road. She fumbled in the pocket of her jacket and retrieved the crumpled piece of paper on which she'd written the names and dates of the men who'd had bikes stolen.

Two of the names on her list of stolen bikes were the same as the poker pizza regulars.

Her heart started beating a little faster. Wasn't it an odd coincidence that two people who were regulars at the poker nights had had bikes stolen? Collin would have known these men would be away ... And thinking about it, she realized Collin had started buying his toys right about the time of the first bike theft ...

The answer came so clearly, she couldn't believe she hadn't thought of it earlier. It was so obvious. Collin Watson was the bike thief!

It seemed bizarre, but she knew Collin wasn't above breaking the law and seriously. He'd gone on to more serious crimes after the stereo theft with Grey. His illegal alcohol possession charges and drunk driving, not to mention his marijuana bust, were common knowledge. If it weren't for his dad, Collin would have been locked up and the key thrown away long ago. Somehow, his dad had always managed to keep him out of jail, but in the process, Collin's contempt for the legal system must have grown. He was always making derogatory comments about the cops not being able to make a bust stick and how he was so much smarter than the police.

Stealing fast bikes and selling them would be Collin's style. It sounded like an exotic crime and the ego boost from outwitting the local cops would be irresistible. It made sense.

And with Collin privy to the poker information, it was a sure thing. If she hadn't been working at the restaurant, she wouldn't have been able to tie the poker pizza together with the victims and Collin. No wonder the cops hadn't come up with that connection — they didn't waitress at Mountain Bistro!

Jan's mind was running at light speed now.

Collin had framed Grey to divert the police.

Grey would have taken Collin's offer to try out the Bimoto, thinking the hotshot owned the bike because Collin could conceivably have bought something that exotic. Then Collin would have anonymously tipped off the cops when Grey was on his ride. The plan would have been to bust Grey, and when he blamed Collin, well, everyone knew Grey had a grudge against the guy. It would look like a guilty Grey was trying to frame poor Collin.

Collin had lucked out when Grey had crashed the bike before he had a chance to implicate him at all. He was completely in the clear until Grey got his memory back and by then Collin would have covered his tracks.

It was imperative she try and jog Grey's memory the next time she saw her brother. It still bothered her that the only part of his story that was a complete blank, was the bike theft. She knew Gellar would say it was very convenient. She pushed those thoughts out of her head. She believed Grey when he told her he couldn't remember the crash, but would the police?

She considered her course of action. She didn't want to tell David her suspicion yet. Not till she had proof of Collin's guilt. The first thing she'd have to do was check around and find out where Collin was when the bike thefts occurred. If she could put him in the right place at the right time to connect him with the thefts, all she had to do was come up with some hard evidence and Sergeant Gellar would have to listen to her. She should also check his whereabouts when she'd been run off the road on the way back from Banff.

This was exciting. The more she thought about it, the more it made sense. However, she would have to be dead sure before she accused Collin or she'd end up in serious trouble herself — especially since Collin's dad and Sergeant Gellar would be involved.

There was one thing she should check. She turned her bike around and headed back to Bragg Creek. Pulling into the parking lot, she parked her bike, then hurried across the pavement and into the office of Bragg Creek Travel.

"Hi, Colleen," she said to the pretty young woman behind the desk. "I was wondering if you could give me some information?" She then explained how she had to send out some bills from the restaurant and needed to know whether either one of these regulars, Jan showed her the two names she'd written on the crumpled paper, had been away recently. She made up an excuse about tabs and an accounting mixup and that she didn't want to overcharge them if they hadn't been around to have their pizzas.

Jan knew it was thin, but Colleen only smiled and said to wait just a minute. She called up the names on her computer.

"Yes, looks like those gentlemen were each gone sometime in the last four months." She said, tapping the screen with her pen.

"Do you suppose I could get the dates they were gone?" Jan asked, smiling innocently at the helpful woman.

"No problem, Jan. If you come around here, I can show you on the screen," Colleen said, sliding her chair so Jan could get a clear view of the computer screen.

Jan went behind the desk and noted the dates on her paper. Collin would have sat in on games, found out when the next man was going away and planned the theft from the information he got at the game. The other thefts were probably just lucky strikes from other information he'd picked up.

Her case against Collin was taking shape.

She thanked Colleen, stuffed the paper back in her coat, and started to leave. Just as she stepped out onto the boardwalk, she saw Collin walking toward her.

"Going on a trip, Jan?" he asked, glancing from her to the travel office.

"It would be nice. Sorry I can't chat, but I've got to run, Collin," she said with a forced smile before hurrying down the steps and across the parking lot to her bike.

She could feel him watching her as she walked away and it made the hair stand up on the back of her neck. Just as she pulled her helmet on, she saw him turn and go into the travel office.

# Chapter 7

Jan wondered why Collin had gone into the travel agency. She had the awful feeling it was to check up on her. If he were the mastermind, he'd be watching for anyone to get wise to him.

She rode home thinking of this new revelation about Collin. It gave her a weird feeling remembering him watching her cross the parking lot. She knew she was right about him and she was going to prove it.

She rolled the whole thing over and over in her mind as she worked the next day. It made sense. The only thing she couldn't understand was why she hadn't thought of it before. Jan was looking forward to telling Josh her theory on Collin's involvement in the motorcycle thefts. He was one person she was sure would agree with her. She'd be gone by the time Josh came in for his shift, but maybe she'd stop by at closing and tell him then.

In the meantime, she would spend her free time checking up on Collin's whereabouts on a few critical days.

She was just coming out of the grocery store when she spotted Zero Chung heading for the bridge that led west out of town. As one of Collin's regular sidekicks, Zero might be a good person to get to know better.

The bridge crossed the Elbow River, which made it confusing for tourists, who assumed the watercourse it spanned was Bragg Creek, which the town was named after. Bragg Creek was a little harder to find. It was a very small tributary, which started high in the foothills west of the town and lazily meandered its way to meet the Elbow. Its path was so twisted, you crossed the small stream three times before you got to Jan's house. It really wasn't much of a creek to look at. More what you'd call quaint, except in spring when the melted snow from the mountains turned it into a respectable torrent.

Zero, however, lived only a short walk from town and crossed just the main bridge over the Elbow. His house was in Elkana Estates and as he had no car of his own, he usually hiked everywhere or rode his mountain bike. Today he was on foot.

"Hey, Zero, wait for me," Jan called, as she hurried to catch the lanky youth. Zero was so tall and thin, he looked like a praying mantis — all stick arms and legs.

"Hi, Jan, what's up?" he asked, slowing his loping gait just a little.

Thinking quickly, Jan thought of her friend who lived further up the road. Visiting her would give Jan an excuse to walk with Zero. "Oh, nothing. I was just heading over to Mary's and I thought I'd walk with you." She grinned at him. "You're not that bad as make-do company goes."

The longhaired young man made a face at her. "Gee, thanks for the compliment, I think. How's Grey?"

"He's still in the ICU, but he's improving," she said evasively. No sense in letting Collin know Grey was awake any sooner than need be. "You know how it is, lots of medical mumbo jumbo."

"Yeah, I know," he said sympathetically. "My aunt has breathing problems from emphysema and uses a portable oxygen tank. The docs are always measuring her oxygen levels. Pretty heavy stuff." He tossed a stick he'd been carrying into the river. It made a satisfying *splunk* as it sliced its way through the surface then bobbed energetically back up four metres downstream.

Jan sighed. "It's scary, but what can you do? It's in higher hands than mine." She thought about this a moment. Did she mean God's hands? She gave herself a mental shake. No, Grey's case was for the guy with the white coat, not the white robes. But when it came right down to it, who really knew? Lately, she'd been wondering about things she'd been sure of before.

She refocused. "Hey, Zero, Collin's new camera was really cool. He must have won the lotto to afford all that loot," she said casually.

Zero grinned. "I don't know how that guy does it. He's never strapped for bucks and he's not stingy with his money either. He's always willing to lend a guy a couple of pesos in between paydays."

"Yeah, he's a prince," Jan said trying to keep the sarcasm out of her voice. "Maybe he's got some new job he hasn't told you about. You know, agent for Her Majesty's Secret Service." She was hoping her attempt at humour would get Zero talking.

"No, I don't think so. I'd know," Zero said seriously, shaking his head.

"You can't know what he does all the time. Maybe it's a weekend job. Take for instance, last Saturday. Was he around then?" she asked.

"Nope, come to think of it, I have no idea where he was. You know, that's kind of strange. I don't remember seeing him at all until later Saturday night." The way he said it, Jan knew he was telling the truth.

"Hey, do you know if Collin's taken up touring in the woods, hiking maybe? From those pictures we saw, I wondered if he spent a lot of time checking out Mother Nature?"

"Nah, Collin hates anything that's green and leafy, stays right away from the woods as much as possible. He hates all this rustic crap," he said, pointing to the deep green, towering pines and weathered wooden fences lining the road. "More of a steel and plastic man," Zero said matter-of-factly.

"Is that so," she said, nodding her head. "I guess you'd know. You're his best friend." She tried another approach. "I thought Collin would have bought another bike by now. He used to like motorbiking. Does he ride anymore?" she asked casually as she watched a couple of mule deer calmly munching on Mrs. Helfrich's lovingly tended flowerbeds.

"He hasn't said anything about biking for a long time. I haven't even seen him on a bike since the accident. You know Collin, what's *then* is forgotten, what's *now* is everything. He's so into that car of his, I don't think he'll ever go back to two wheels." He laughed.

They'd reached Mary's driveway. "This is my stop," she said. "See you next time you need a Bragg Special and an orange pop." She winked at Zero and began walking down the long driveway to her friend's house. She didn't even know if Mary was home, and she didn't want to find out. As soon as she was out of sight of the pathway, she stopped and dodged behind one of the pines that lined the roadway. The thick branches effectively screened her from both the house and the pathway. She needn't have worried. Zero never looked back.

Once she was sure he was out of sight, Jan started back toward town. Bumping into Zero had really paid off in information. Collin hadn't been around on Saturday when the whole Banff thing had happened and to be that far into the bush just to take a picture of a cairn wasn't his style. And just because Zero hadn't seen him on a bike, didn't mean he wasn't the thief, only that he was being an extra-careful thief.

It wasn't what Sergeant Gellar would call hard evidence that Collin was the Lightning Rider, but it put him well within the realm of possibility. Jan was even more convinced her instincts were right.

* * *

The next morning Jan was just finishing topping up her gas tank at the local Husky gas station, when she noticed Collin pull in around behind the building to the service bays. His Camaro was hard to miss with its custom paint job.

She had tried to catch Josh at the restaurant last night to tell him her news, but Robin had taken pity on him and let him leave early. Jan was too shy to call him at home. She'd tell him the first chance she got.

She went inside to pay and as she waited at the till, she heard Collin talking with Don Zadnik, the mechanic, in the work bay. They were discussing whether Collin could get his flat tire fixed now or wait his turn. Collin wasn't good at waiting. Jan knew this from being his server at the restaurant. She heard him say he would get the tire out of his trunk and she watched him go back out to his car.

"The gas was $5.00, Don," she called into the cavernous work bay. "The money's on the counter."

"Okay, Jan, thanks," Don said, heading back up to the front of the service station and the cash register.

She left the garage and quickly walked to her bike. Starting her machine, she zipped nimbly around the gas pumps and doubled back to where she could see Collin's car.

She parked her bike out of sight at the end of the building and peered around the corner to where Collin's car sat gleaming in the bright sunshine. As she pulled her helmet off, she could hear Collin back inside the bay with the damaged tire arguing with Don.

Quickly, she walked over to the car. Scanning the interior, she could see no incriminating evidence. She really hadn't expected to see any, but a girl can occasionally get lucky.

She kept glancing at the service bay door for any sign of Collin.

Opening the passenger door, she noted the keys were not in the ignition. Quickly, Jan searched for the trunk release button. It wasn't anywhere she could see or feel under the dash.

She had a sudden inspiration. Flipping open the glove compartment, she reached inside.

The box itself held a small cell phone and several unpaid parking tickets along with the car's registration and insurance, which were in a pink card holder. Just inside the outer edge of the compartment, there were two switches. She tried one, and nothing happened, but when she pressed the other, she heard a soft click as the hatchback released.

Quietly, she closed the passenger door. And, checking for Collin, moved quickly to the back of the car.

Her heart was pounding as she opened the trunk and looked in. She wasn't sure what she expected to find, but it wasn't what she saw.

The trunk was completely empty. She remembered Collin wasn't known for his sentimentality. Once he was through with something or someone, it was instantly ancient history. The absence of any form of emergency

102

equipment like jumper cables or tools also said something about his casual approach to life skills. It was obvious he'd never been a Boy Scout or caught with a dead battery in a howling snow storm twenty kilometres from home.

If the car broke down, Collin would just call someone on his cell phone, then abandon the car. It would usually end up on a tow truck hook. She wondered who'd put the spare on his Camaro. She didn't think Collin even knew where the jack was.

She was just going to close the trunk, when the thought of a jack gave her an idea. The spare tire was usually tucked away in a small compartment under the trunk floor mat.

She found the snaps that held the carpet down and pulled. The spare tire well had no tire in it, but what it did have was even better. There, neatly folded in the bottom of the recess, were a black leather jacket and matching pants. There was no helmet.

They might have been Collin's old riding leathers from before he had the big crash on his bike. But if they were, why had he kept them after he'd sold the bike? He'd have had no use for them. And why were they secreted away in the bottom of his trunk? It didn't add up — unless he still needed those leathers and she knew exactly the job he'd use them on. This was another piece of hard evidence which, when combined with everything else, made Collin a way more convincing suspect for the bike thefts than Grey. Even Sergeant Gellar would have to concede that.

A noise from the direction of the garage made her look up. Collin was on his way back. Hurriedly, she replaced the well cover and closed the hatch.

She ran for her bike, hoping she hadn't left any trace of her search. From her vantage point around the corner, she watched as Collin stomped back to his car. She guessed he'd been unsuccessful convincing Don how important Collin Watson really was.

She was just doing up her helmet when she heard the Camaro roar to life. The engine noise reverberated off the garage walls like thunder down a canyon. Jan was sure it was revved well into the red zone on the tachometer.

He was going to do one of his famous burnouts that left enough rubber to retread most people's winter tires.

She heard him slam the car into gear, then nothing. He just shot past her and out into the parking lot without the usual deafening squeal. Apparently, Collin wasn't into burnouts today.

She watched as he cranked the wheels sharply. The rear tires locked up in what had to be a hand brake turn. The back end swung in a tight arc as the Camaro came to a sudden stop facing directly at her. Their eyes locked for a split second as recognition flooded across his face. Recognition, and Jan thought, something else. Whatever it was, it sent a shiver down her back.

Jan kicked her bike over and headed out of the lot.

She buzzed up through the gears, accelerating up the south road and out of town. At the junction of Highway 66 and Highway 22 she saw Constable McKenna setting up his photo radar. Pulling over, she shut off her engine and waved.

"Hi there, Jan, what's up?" he asked, smiling at her.

"Hey, David," she said flipping her helmet visor open. "I was just wondering if you've noticed anything odd about Collin Watson lately?" She knew it was a weird question, but she wasn't sure how else to ask.

"By odd, do you mean odder than his usual behaviour or do you have something particular in mind?" he asked.

"I was thinking odd even for Collin, something that might have triggered alarm bells in a good cop like yourself," she said helpfully.

He thought a moment. "This wouldn't have anything to do with your brother's case would it? You remember, the one you were going to leave in police hands."

"I know I'm not supposed to interfere in a police investigation, but from where I stand there doesn't seem to be much of an investigation. In fact, all I'm doing is keeping the book from being closed on Grey entirely." She crossed her arms. "In fact," she said rather more loudly than she had intended, "it's starting to resemble a good old-fashioned lynching party and Sergeant Gellar's got the rope."

"Whoa now, I'm on your side, remember?" He stopped what he was doing. "Jan, I know it looks bad for Grey. I'm not saying it doesn't, but no one wants the wrong person jailed for this — no one, including Sergeant Gellar. If you know something, I'd consider it a personal favour if you'd let me help."

Jan knew she couldn't tell David about her suspicions until she had more solid evidence.

"Look, I'm working on a theory, and I just need to know I can count on you if I need to."

David nodded his head. "You can always count on me, but you have to remember, Jan, I have to obey the law just like everyone else. And the law says you are innocent until proven guilty — that includes Collin Watson. Without proof, he's considered innocent in the eyes of the law."

"Okay, but if you notice him doing anything strange, couldn't you look into it a little closer than you would normally? Where there's smoke there's fire, David." She hoped he understood what she was trying to say.

He smiled at her. "You know, there have been a couple of times I've noticed Collin heading west in that hot car of his, then return later with another vehicle right behind him, sometimes quite late at night. I thought it was odd because you don't see much traffic on this road late at night, and two vehicles in a row is very unlikely unless they know each other."

He finished hooking up his camera. "Maybe the next time I see our young lad coming back from K-Country accompanied by a stranger, I'll just pull them both over and have a chat. I'm not saying Collin did it, Jan. I want to be clear on that. He's still innocent until proven guilty, but I will keep a weather eye on our boy." He started walking back over to his car. "And Jan, remember, leave police business to the police."

"You bet. Consider me just another concerned citizen with a couple of observations that might help your official investigation." She grinned at him, then added, "Oh, and David — thanks. All I've ever asked is that the police keep an open mind about Grey. Don't write him off yet."

She got back on her bike feeling better than she had since this whole thing had started.

* * *

When she got back home, her mom was waiting to go to the hospital. Jan quickly changed and went with her mom.

She was in such a good mood as they visited Grey. Jan spent most of the time telling them jokes she'd heard at the restaurant.

"January, I don't know how you do it. I have enough trouble retelling just one joke with the punch line in the right place," her mom said, shaking her head. "How

106

would it be if I go to the cafeteria and get us all milk-shakes?" she offered.

Both Jan and her brother agreed that was just what the party needed. Her mom left with instructions for a chocolate for Grey and a strawberry for Jan.

Once she'd left, Jan decided it was time to see if Grey remembered any more about the crash.

"Grey, I was wondering if any details have come back about who gave you the bike? Can you remember anything, anything at all?" she asked.

Grey looked at his sister and shook his head slowly. "I told you, nothing. I wish I could."

"The problem is it looks really bad, like you're either protecting someone or trying to get out of it yourself. Grey, I want to help you, but I need something to go on." She saw the hurt look in her brother's eyes. Squeezing his hand, she added, "Just try to remember, that's all I ask." She smiled at him and changed the subject.

She knew she was going to have to get to the bottom of this alone.

* * *

Josh was just getting ready to close when Jan dropped by the restaurant.

"I need to talk to you. I think I know who the bike thief is and you're going to like it." She thought he looked good for having just worked a long shift. His straight brown hair was getting long enough to need a cut soon. She liked the way he wore it super short.

"Your timing's perfect. I was just going to pull my supper out of the oven. We can eat while you tell me what's up. You get the pop. I'll get our pizza." He started toward the large pizza oven that was at the back of the kitchen.

Jan poured the drinks and, grabbing a couple of plates, headed to the staff table.

Once they were settled, Josh dished out large slices of pepperoni and mushroom pizza with extra cheese onto two plates.

"So, what's the scoop?" he asked, taking a huge bite.

Jan was too excited to eat. "I know who stole the bikes," she said, smiling at Josh.

He stopped in midchew, then asked with his mouth still full, "Who, for crying out loud?"

"Collin Watson," she said with satisfaction.

Josh stopped chewing. "That would be a treat," he said, grinning. "But wishing it so and having it so are two different things. What makes you so sure about Collin?" He took a long drink of his pop, then continued attacking his pizza.

Jan cut a small piece off her slice of pizza and picked it up with her fork. "First there's the matter of all the spare cash he's come up with. He doesn't work and his dad won't give him any money since keeping Collin out of jail is turning out to be a full-time job. If he charged his son for legal fees, it would make the national debt look small." She ate the tempting morsel, enjoying the intimate feeling she got sitting here with Josh, alone.

"Then, I've been doing some checking and you know the poker pizza crowd, well a couple of them are on the theft list. The neat tie-in is that Collin fills in for the missing player and yaks with the other men. How hard would it be for him to find out what bikes they ride and when they're going out of town? I checked the timing on the thefts. There's also the Banff fiasco. His whereabouts are unknown for a lot of the times in question and, because he doesn't have a job, he has plenty of opportunity to heist those bikes during the day when most people are at work." She grinned in satisfaction. "I'm right on this one, Josh. All I need to do is prove it."

"Yeah, so he has a lot of free time, that's the truth and he does seem to have a lot of cash for a spoilt kid who never had to work a day in his life. But don't you have to have solid proof to nail him for something as big as this?" Josh asked, wiping his mouth with the back of his hand, then taking another bite.

This wasn't the response she'd expected. Oddly, she felt as though she had to defend her accusation of Collin, and to Josh of all people! She'd thought he'd have wanted Collin to be the guilty party, no questions asked.

"I do," she said, still a little irritated at having to defend her idea. She went on enthusiastically. "He also has in his possession, hidden in his car, a set of black motorcycle leathers just like the ones the guy who ran my mom and me off the road wore and just like the ones the guy in Banff had on and like a rider seen fleeing from the scene of one of the bike thefts. I'm telling you, Collin Watson is the guy." She sat back, content in her flawless logic and sipped on her pop.

Josh looked at her in surprise. "It was you Collin was talking about when he was in earlier. He said he knew someone had been snooping in his car because they'd switched on the traction control and he couldn't do a burnout in the parking lot. He said if he ever caught this person, he'd straighten the matter out himself."

Jan looked a little sheepish. "Who knew? I had to check out his car and I couldn't find the stupid trunk release. These newfangled gadgets are a pain in the butt," she said in her best cowgirl twang. "However, this does mean Collin knows I'm on to him, and after the Banff trip, I know he's dangerous."

"What about the lightning bolt helmet that Collin wore in all three incidents? You need that helmet to clinch the case. That piece is crucial or it's no deal. His dad will just get him off again," Josh said as he finished off his fifth piece.

"Unless Grey can ID Collin as the guy who gave him the Bimota," she said confidently. "He still can't remember anything about the crash, but once he does get his memory back, Grey will tell the cops it was Collin who gave him that bike. Then they get a search warrant, find the leathers and the helmet stashed at Collin's house somewhere and Wham! One airtight case. Collin's so arrogant, he won't get rid of the evidence because he doesn't think he'll ever get caught, or that the police are smart enough to find the stuff even if he is. He has that big an ego." She pushed her plate away.

She felt really good. She was sure she was right and soon, if everything went the way she planned, the real culprit would finally be put away.

"I don't know, Jan. It still sounds iffy. Maybe you should chill for a while. Wait and see what happens next. You know, Collin may tip his hand. After all, Grey still can't clear himself." He reached for the last piece. "I sure wouldn't go to the cops, if I were you. Not till you have that punk Watson dead to rights."

"Yeah, I know." Again Jan felt a fleeting irritation with Josh. "Besides, I think Grey should be the one to start things rolling with the police. If I go to Gellar, he's going to think this is just a smear campaign by the Métis girl. No, Grey should speak up first, then I can go to the authorities and tell them how I think Collin ties in to the big picture. I'll wait. I'm sure Grey's memory will come back any time now." She hoped she sounded a lot more confident on this point than she felt.

"You know what, January Fournier?" Josh asked, grinning at her. "I think any bad guys in the area should be really worried if you're on the case. You've got brains." His eyes narrowed when he looked at her, "and you use them."

Jan could feel herself blushing. She felt oddly uneasy under his glowing praise.

# Chapter 8

As Jan and her mom walked through the crowded lobby of the hospital, Jan thought how odd it was that she now was used to the hustle and bustle of a busy metropolitan hospital. In fact, she was actually starting to see organization and patterns to the apparent chaos when they were in the ICU.

To the uninitiated, the hectic interplay of nurses and doctors, respiratory therapists and blood techs would be hard to understand, but to Jan, it had turned into routine. Often when they were visiting Grey, they would have to leave for a short time while the doctors examined him. Jan and her mom would sometimes go to the waiting room where Jan would read *National Geographics*, some from as far back as 1982, or just wait outside his room until the doctors were finished. While they were waiting, Jan would watch the staff as they worked. Sometimes the constant ebb and flow of their interaction was so smooth it seemed choreographed.

Jan wasn't as nervous about all the hardware anymore either. She'd studied the dials and traces and, after asking the nurses a few pertinent questions, now knew what most of the different coloured lines meant. At a glance she could see if any of Grey's vitals had changed. It allowed her to ask more intelligent questions of the highly trained staff who cared for her brother.

They'd just entered the ICU, when Jan thought she noticed more than the usual activity coming and going from Grey's room. As they got closer, her heart started beating just a little faster as warning bells went off in her head.

Something was wrong. This was not normal.

"I think there's something going on, Mom," she said as they approached.

Her mom then became aware of the heightened activity also. She quickened her pace.

They stood at the door to Grey's room and looked inside. There were doctors and nurses hovering over Grey, who looked unconscious on the bed.

Jan stopped Susan, who she knew was Grey's nurse, as she came out of his room.

"Susan, what's going on?" Jan asked apprehensively.

"Has something happened to Grey?" her mom asked. Her voice sounded controlled, but Jan heard the anxiety just below the calm words.

Susan hesitated, then seeing the worry in the older woman's eyes, nodded. "Actually, yes, Mrs. Fournier, there's been an ... incident." The nurse sounded somewhat flustered, which was very odd for her, as the nurses Jan had seen always appeared to be in complete control of the situation.

"What do you mean an *incident*?" Jan asked apprehensively.

"Perhaps Dr. Singh should explain. If you'll have a seat in the family room, he'll be in to see you in a moment." She smiled at Jan and her mom, but it did little to allay Jan's fears.

"Is my son all right?" Jan's mom asked. The tone in her voice alerted the nurse that this was no time for the usual platitudes and delaying tactics.

She nodded. "Yes, he's stable, but he did have a ..." she paused, "small crisis. If you'll please wait in the family room Mrs. Fournier ..."

Her mom sighed with relief. "Thank you for the information, Susan. Please ask the doctor to come in as soon as he's through with Grey." She turned and walked toward the softly lit room that she and Jan had become so familiar with.

Jan nodded at Susan and followed her mom.

Jan sat next to her mom and settled in for the standard twenty-minute wait. She was surprised when Dr. Singh walked through the door a couple of minutes later.

They both looked up as he entered.

"Mrs. Fournier, Jan," he said, sitting in a chair opposite Jan and her mom. "Grey's had a bit of a setback, but he's stable now and resting."

"What kind of a setback, Doctor?" her mom asked anxiously.

Jan sensed there was more to this than he wanted to say.

"I think you'd better tell us what happened." She looked pointedly at the doctor and Jan could see he knew he'd better come clean.

Dr. Singh gathered his thoughts, then began. "It seems Grey had a visitor, a Sergeant Gellar, who told the ward clerk he wanted to speak with the patient. The ward clerk explained Grey was still very weak, but the officer was very insistent, claiming an official investigation was ongoing." He shook his head knowingly. "The ward clerk then asked Sergeant Gellar to wait in the family room while she got someone who could speak with him about Grey's case. While she was looking for a staff member, Sergeant Gellar took it upon himself to go to Grey's room and interrogate him. The nurse could hear the Sergeant speaking very loudly, something about not getting away with it by faking

114

amnesia. It appears Grey's response to the questioning was …" he said, looking for the right word, "negative."

Her mother looked surprised. "You mean his life could have been endangered by Sergeant Gellar's actions?" her mom asked in a controlled voice, but Jan could see her getting more and more angry as the story came out.

"We don't think it went that far. Susan interceded and insisted that the officer leave. There was a problem at that time, and an orderly was called in, at which point the sergeant left, saying he would return." He sat back in his chair. "Grey's reactions to the questioning brought on a heightened degree of respiratory and cardiac distress, but he's sedated now and resting comfortably. His vitals are coming back to normal."

Jan cleared her throat. "He's going to be okay, right?"

Dr. Singh pursed his lips. "We feel the incident may have weakened Grey, but we're optimistic he'll regain the ground he lost very quickly. However, I have to be honest with you, Mrs. Fournier, I wouldn't advise allowing Sergeant Gellar to question Grey again until he's a lot stronger. It could be dangerous." He saw the look on Jan's face. "He's sleeping, but you could go and see him if you like, just to put your minds at ease."

Jan nodded as she and her mom stood up.

"We'd like that, Doctor."

Together, they walked toward his room. Her mother had her rosary in her hand. For some reason, this made Jan feel better. It was one of her mom's ways of coping and Jan wanted her mom to be able to cope. If a string of well-worn beads helped, Jan was all for it.

Her brother looked grey and shrunken as he lay sleeping. The bandages on his head made his face look small and, somehow, vulnerable. All the optimism Jan had felt the last time she'd seen her brother evaporated as she watched his laboured breathing.

They only stayed a short time before her mom said they were leaving.

The drive home was quiet, but every now and then her mom would look at Jan and smile reassuringly. They drove directly to the police station at Bragg Creek.

"I'd like to speak to Sergeant Gellar," her mom said to the officer working at the front desk.

"He's in his office. If you'd have a seat, I'll tell him you're here. Your name is Mrs. ..."

"Fournier, and I'll tell him myself," she said as she pushed through the side gate and walked directly to Gellar's office.

The officer behind the desk began protesting, but it was too late.

Jan watched in amazement as her mom opened the door and marched into Gellar's office, firmly closing the door behind her.

Even through the closed door, Jan could hear their raised voices. Gellar yelling how he was well within the law in questioning a suspect, especially one with a history, countered by her mom's strong calm voice speaking about the repercussions of questioning her son when he was still so ill.

Jan was surprised when she realized she'd never heard her mom speak with this kind of anger before. It was *cool!* Jan didn't think Sergeant Gellar would soon forget his chat with her mom. She waited until, a couple of minutes later, her mom walked sedately out of Gellar's office and over to Jan.

"Let's go, January." Her mom said quietly as she walked past, her head held high.

Jan didn't argue.

Jan didn't need to ask what had transpired in Gellar's office. She found herself smiling all the way home.

One thing was for certain, she wasn't going to even suggest Collin Watson be brought in for questioning until she had him cold. After today, Jan doubted that Sergeant Gellar would tolerate anything less than concrete proof from the Métis girl.

# Chapter 9

That evening, David McKenna came over to their house. He'd called with some questions about Grey's case just as they'd arrived home from the police station and Jan's mom took the opportunity to invite him over for supper when he could ask both of them his questions.

Jan helped her mom in the kitchen preparing the meal. After the visit to Sergeant Gellar's office, Jan felt like she and her mom shared some kind of secret. It was as though she had this other mom, one who was a real tiger when her cubs were threatened. Jan liked it. It made her feel safe and secure.

After they finished their meal, she cleared the table and told her mom to go sit in the living room with Constable McKenna while she put the tea on.

Jan had decided on the ride home today that she was going to do something drastic to try and get the ball rolling on proving Collin's guilt.

Collin's dad was a very good lawyer and used to getting his son out of all sorts of trouble. Without tangible proof, he wouldn't have any problem tearing apart Jan's allegations considering Collin's and Grey's history.

Jan put the teapot and cups on a tray with the milk and sugar. She also cut two slices of the homemade Prizefighter Pie they'd picked up from Karen's Pie Shop as they'd driven through Bragg Creek on their way home. The big blueberries and blackberries made an awesome combination and it was Jan's personal favourite from the many exotic varieties offered at the popular dessert shop.

When she walked into the living room, David was just stoking up the fire. It had begun to rain as they'd driven home today, and up here in the high foothills, the rain was very cold and even in the summer, could turn to snow. The fire was cheery and made the room warm and inviting. Jan set the tray down in front of her mom.

"Aren't you going to have any pie with us, honey?" her mom asked as Jan turned to go back to the kitchen.

"Actually, Mom, I think I'll take my piece up to my room. I want to finish a book and unless David, I mean *Constable McKenna* has any questions for me …" She looked at him inquiringly, but he shook his head.

"None that can't wait, Jan, it's okay." He smiled at her. "You're off the hook."

She grinned back at David. She'd suspected he didn't really have any questions for them when he'd called this afternoon. "There's more pie in the kitchen, Constable. Don't worry about your waistline, just help yourself." She left before David could say anything.

Later, when Jan took her plate down to the kitchen, she saw her mom and David sitting on the couch, just watching the fire as the embers glowed in the hearth. Her mom had put some music on. They were listening to Jan's favourite CD, called *Matriarch — Iroquois Women's Songs*. It was by Joanne Shenandoah, an Oneida woman from New York State. Jan loved the background for this recording.

The Oneida were part of the Haudenosaunee Confederacy and their culture believed that women, as lifegivers, were custodians of Mother Earth. This album was a tribute to the women of Ms. Shenandoah's band, who were the spiritual advisors, political counselors and healers of her people. The vocalist's lilting voice was absolutely haunting as she sang about the women of her clan.

Jan could feel the peace in the room. She quietly finished putting her plate away, then went back upstairs.

\* \* \*

The next day she stopped by the police department on her way to the restaurant. All night long she'd thought about Grey and how his life had been turned upside down. If she were right, it was due largely to Collin Watson and she couldn't, wouldn't, let him get away with it. She'd decided she had to take David into her confidence and try to get bigger guns on her side.

David had said he was working in the morning. Jan hoped he would be in the office so she could tell him her suspicions.

"Is Constable McKenna in?" she asked the officer behind the desk.

"As a matter of fact, I am," David said, walking out of an office at the back of the room. "What can I do for you, Jan?" he asked, smiling as he placed a folder in a basket marked *Current Cases*.

"Can we talk, David?" she asked.

"Sure, come on in." He motioned her through the side gate that separated the public area from the officers' work section. "We can talk in here." He opened the door to the office he'd just come out of. Jan followed him in.

"What's up?" he asked.

"Well, I'm really close to putting together a case against Collin. I may need your help." She put up her hand. "I know Mom told you about Sergeant Gellar's visit to the hospital yesterday and how it hurt Grey. I'm going to get this wrapped up once and for all so Grey doesn't have to go through that kind of ordeal again." She never raised her voice, but she thought she heard some of her mom's quiet authority echoing behind her words.

"Jan, I'd like nothing better than to prove Grey's innocence, but we need concrete evidence, not vague hunches and coincidences." He shook his head.

"There is something else ..." she said, debating whether to go on. "I did find some solid evidence — a set of black riding leathers hidden in Collin's car, but they may be gone because I think Collin may have figured out I saw them." David raised an eyebrow at this, but Jan kept on. "Then there's the poker pizza connection ..." She took a deep breath and explained everything she'd put together as David sat quietly listening.

"Jan, if you're right about this, it's gone way past your gathering evidence. I think we have to bring Sergeant Gellar in on it. He's my superior officer and can authorize the procedures we need, like search warrants."

Her response was immediate and definite. "No!" David's eyebrows shot up. She quickly tried to explain her reaction. "I mean, I don't think that would do any good. You and I both know he wants Grey to go to jail for these thefts. He's not going to help us pin this on a nice white kid like Collin."

David gave her a warning look. "You're letting the past cloud your judgement. We need the full force of the law behind us if we're to go ahead. Without following the right legal steps, even if we do nail Collin, it wouldn't stick. His dad would get him off again on a technicality — not following proper police procedures."

Jan thought about this. It went against her gut instincts, but she nodded her head. If it meant keeping David on her side, she was willing to let Gellar know what she'd found out. She sighed and relented, seeing the logic of what David had said. "Okay, if it means clearing Grey, I'll do it."

David left the office for a few minutes and returned with Sergeant Gellar.

"What's this Constable McKenna tells me about you making a serious accusation against Collin Watson with not a shred of hard evidence to back it up?" he asked the second he entered the room. "If this is another of your concocted stories, this time I'll charge you myself."

David sat beside her, which made Jan feel much better. After yesterday, she didn't think the Fourniers were high on the sergeant's list.

She sat up straighter in her chair. "It's not a story. I think there's enough weird stuff here to switch the focus of your investigation from my brother to Collin Watson." As she went on to explain her suspicions, she chose her words carefully and tried to keep her voice controlled, but found it kept increasing in volume on its own. "And I know you think if Grey's tied into one bike theft, that would automatically make him the prime suspect in all the other thefts that have happened around here lately," she finished, feeling her temper rising along with her voice.

David interjected, trying to calm things down. "I agree with the sergeant; there is nothing concrete." He turned to Gellar. "However, when viewed as a body of evidence, Sergeant, I think there is enough here to warrant further investigation of Collin Watson."

Sergeant Gellar's usually pallid complexion looked red and mottled in the dull glow of the fluorescent light. Jan could see a vein throbbing in his temple.

When he spoke, his voice was low and menacing. "I will personally take over this inquiry, Constable. I'm not about to embarrass a prominent family with wild accusations and unsubstantiated allegations made by ..." His eyes narrowed as he looked at Jan. "The interfering sister of an Indian kid who was caught red-handed with the stolen bike and who has *conveniently* forgotten where he got the bike from!" He practically spat the words out.

David's chair teetered precariously as he shot to his feet and Jan could see the anger flash in his eyes.

Gellar went on before David could say anything. "And if I feel my authority is being challenged or compromised in any way, you will answer directly to me and I will make sure you are reassigned to more appropriate duty. Is that clear, Constable?" He glared at David.

"Yes, *sir*," David said in a tight voice.

With that, Gellar turned and strode out of the room, slamming the door behind him.

David shoved his chair against the table. "I don't know how he got to where he is. He's such a redneck son of a ..." He expelled his breath in a rush. "Look, Jan, we have to make the best of this. The good thing is now Gellar has to check out your theory. It's not just a *Métis girl* this time, it's a white cop too."

He smiled reassuringly at her, but Jan was not so sure. She thought a man like Gellar could make a lot of things go away if he wanted to and she was sure this would be one case that he would want to make disappear.

"Are you going to back off like Gellar wants?" she asked accusingly.

David looked at her and shook his head. "Don't worry. Haven't you ever heard the expression *We always get our man*?"

Jan smiled weakly. "I thought that was the Mounties," she said, rising and picking up her motorcycle helmet.

They both started out of the office together. "Was it?" David said in mock surprise. "Well, it's a darn good idea, whoever said it." He walked her out to the main desk. "Don't worry, Jan. I'll make sure Collin is checked out properly. In fact, it's now number one on my hit list of things to do. I'll start looking into his files. Who knows, he may have a couple of pals from previous busts who need looking up."

Jan left not knowing if this had been a positive meeting or not. She doubted Gellar would go out of his way to nail Collin, but David had been in on the meeting and would be a witness if any of this went to court. When Collin was caught, Gellar would have a lot of explaining to do if he did nothing. However, she still wasn't sure things would work out without her help and, considering the stakes, she wasn't about to find out.

* * *

She had a couple of days off and was polishing her bike, trying not to wince when she rubbed the bruised gas tank. Keeping her bike clean was her way of making everything all right. She was sure if she could just shine the bike enough, Grey would be okay. She was looking forward to trying to find out more about Collin and his mystery money. She knew the cash came from the sale of the bikes, but she needed to understand his system. What was he doing that no one even suspected him or ever saw him?

She decided to approach the problem logically, from beginning to end. He spent money like it was water, so he'd need a constant supply to maintain his cash flow.

He must have a pretty good modus operandi worked out to pull so many thefts off and not get caught.

He'd need to get information about his prospective victims, that's where the poker came in. He'd find out everything he could about the players and their friends — what kind of bikes they owned, where they lived, when they would be away — and no one would be the wiser. Then he'd have to hide the bikes somewhere until he could fence them. The actual selling would have to take place somewhere safe where no one would see him or the fence. It was a complicated plan for one guy, but Collin would love the idea of besting the cops while continuing the thefts right under their noses.

Doing all this without raising suspicion would be tricky in a town this small. He was well known in the area. And the Creek gossip mill would soon spread the word if he were seen with a lot of strange bikes. No, he would have to have a safe house where he wouldn't have to worry about prying and snooping.

She thought about this. There was something in the back of her mind that kept nudging at her brain. Something important she'd forgotten about.

Then it hit her.

Those pictures Collin had shown her. The deliberate attempt to mislead her about the one with the cairn marking John Ware's homestead. It wasn't the cairn he was worried about. It was the old, deserted line shack in the background!

She'd remembered she thought it odd at the time that he would make such a huge logistical mistake about where the cairn was located. The mistake had been leaving the picture in with the others. That line shack would be a perfect hideout. Remote, isolated, but only a fifteen-minute ride from Bragg Creek. It made perfect sense. She threw her wax rag back into a plastic bag.

Glancing at the threatening bank of clouds rolling in from the west, she made a decision. If she left now, she would be able to ride out to the shack and have a look around before any serious weather happened. They were due for a good hailstorm and she didn't feel like riding home on a highway covered with tiny ball bearings.

She hurriedly stashed her cleaning gear in the garage and took her helmet and jacket out of the house. As she pulled her helmet on, she thought of calling David with her latest idea. He was busy checking for any leads from Collin's past that could be important. She'd check the line shack first, then tell him about the picture. In a matter of minutes, she was driving through Bragg Creek on her way to the Kananaskis.

The day was warm, the air still and latent with the threat of foul weather not far off. Everything was simmering in the smoldering summer afternoon. She sliced cleanly through the shimmering air as the heat waves distorted the road ahead.

She watched for the turnoff to the cairn. It was easy to miss, as there was no roadside marker to direct tourists to the little-known site. She dropped down through the gears as she approached the side road.

The dusty road was not in the best repair and she had to keep her speed down to avoid a wipeout. At last she spotted the modest stone cairn beside a fork in the road. She parked her bike on the shoulder and circled around to approach the derelict line shack from the safety of a screen of trees.

The cabin appeared to be deserted as she cautiously moved closer to the dilapidated wooden structure. It looked like it hadn't been used for a long time. The windows had creaky wooden shutters, which banged in the light wind that had sprung up and remnants of an abandoned bird's nest straggled out the top of the old stone chimney. The worn wooden steps up to the front door were broken and a couple had gaping holes through them, making the footing dangerous.

Jan carefully picked her way up the rickety steps and peered through the glassless gaping windows

The inside was dark and dusty. It was hard to tell if it had been used recently as the wind obviously blew fresh dirt in on a regular basis. Jan worked her way around the cabin to the back. The road continued behind the dilapidated shack to another smaller shed. Jan headed for it.

As she made her way to the shed, she noticed tire tracks leading up to an old wooden door that was nailed shut. Her breath caught as she recognized them. They were bike tracks.

She gingerly pulled on the board, which had been loosely nailed across the door. One good yank and it came off in her hands. She was excited now, and a little scared. Jan looked around and listened. All she could hear was the whispering of the wind in the pines and the only things moving were some Appaloosa horses pastured across the road.

Gently, she pulled on the old door. It creaked and gave, opening just enough for her to peek in. A sudden gust of wind blew dust into her eyes, making tears start and reminding her of the impending bad weather.

When she wiped her eyes and looked into the old shed, she couldn't believe what she saw. It was the Honda CBR 900RR Fireblade! The same one that had ridden her off the highway coming back from Banff.

Her hand shook as she held the rickety door open. This was it! Sergeant Gellar had to listen now. This was the proof she needed. All the police had to do was stake the place out and wait for Collin to come and pick up the bike.

She was so excited she couldn't believe her luck! She carefully closed the door, making sure she wedged the nailed board back into place and raced back to her bike.

She'd barely had time to do up her helmet, when the clouds opened up and the storm hit.

She decided to take a shortcut back that she and Grey had found one day when they were out exploring the maze of little-used roads that crisscrossed the back country around this area. It was shorter and would save her time, but the old paved road wasn't used anymore since they'd opened the new wide two-lane, and was in poor shape. The ride would be tricky, especially in the rain and hail. The rutted road was full of potholes and she had to be extremely careful she didn't lose control.

The cold rain pelted her and she was very glad her mom's Christmas present had been the gauntlets she now wore. The tough leather protected her hands from the stinging beads that sliced their way out of the sky.

She'd just come around a tight blind corner, being careful to stay exactly on the racing line, when she saw the washout. The whole paved surface was gone across nearly the entire width of the roadway and a wide gaping hole was all that was left. She barely had time to swerve and cut to the inside line to avoid dumping the bike and herself down the steep washed-out ravine.

If she hadn't been going so slowly because of the rain, she'd have driven right into it. She was shaken at the near miss and felt relieved when the disused side road joined the main highway.

The rest of the ride was cold, but she made better time, and as the freezing rain pelted at her, Jan decided heated handlebar grips would make a nice present for next Christmas. She rode straight to the police station. As she climbed stiffly off her bike, she felt excited. Sergeant Gellar had to believe her this time.

"I need to talk to Sergeant Gellar. It's important," she said before the officer behind the desk had a chance to ask her why she was there. Rainwater pooled around her boots, forming two muddy little puddles where she stood.

"I'm sorry, miss, but he's not in today. Is there some-one else who could help you?" the officer asked.

Jan knew there was only one other person who could help. "Is Constable McKenna here?" she asked, trying to be patient.

The officer smiled at Jan. "Actually, you can prob-ably catch him at Robin's. He's at lunch."

Jan was already heading out the door. "Thanks," she called over her shoulder.

She burst into the restaurant and glanced around. No David.

Josh was in the kitchen and she headed toward the swinging doors.

"Hi, I found something that will help our case. I need to find David McKenna, do you know where he went?" she asked Josh, who had looked up as she came bursting into the kitchen.

"Ah, well, he was here earlier. What's up? What did you find out about Collin?" He looked around the kitchen to make sure the bus person was still out front.

"The best news for Grey," she said breathlessly. "You'll never believe this, but the CBR that rode me into the ditch — I found it. It's hidden in a shed up at a line shack by John Ware's cairn. It's the same bike! I need David to go up with me and see the evidence, and then the cops can stake the place out and pick up Collin when he comes for the bike. It's Grey's ticket out of trouble. Oh, Josh, isn't it great?" She was really excited now.

"You're kidding!" Josh said, a look of shocked surprise on his face. This is great news, Jan. Heck, this is just what you need to put Collin away." He thought a minute. "I heard McKenna say he was going to NoKaOi Ranch after lunch. You may be able to catch him if you hurry." He grinned at her. "You're quite the Sherlock Holmes."

Jan grinned back at him. "And you're my Watson. I'll get David and we can start back right now." She headed out of the restaurant.

"Let me know what happens." Josh called to her retreating back.

Jan ran down the steps to the parking lot. The rain wasn't letting up much. She looked to the west, but could see no break in the heavy grey clouds. In a minute she was on her bike and heading over the bridge on her way out of town. NoKaOi wasn't that far away, but in the rain, she couldn't push her bike too hard. She slowed down to what seemed a crawl. The pavement was greasy and slick and she didn't want any delays due to wipeouts. The trip was taking an eternity now.

When she got to the main house at NoKaOi, she noted there was no police car parked in the front. Not a good sign, she thought, as she raced up the steps.

A pleasant-looking woman with a long brown braid down the middle of her back and a faded denim shirt answered the door.

"I'm looking for Constable McKenna and was told he was coming out here. Do you know where I can find him?" she asked, somewhat breathlessly.

The woman shook her head. "He was out here this morning, but he left before lunch. I think he said he was going to the old Elkana ranch this afternoon."

But Josh had said he heard David say he was coming out here after lunch. This mixup was costing her time.

Jan thanked the woman and climbed back on her bike. She was thoroughly drenched now and the cold was starting to seep into her bones.

She pushed her bike a little harder than good judgement and poor roads said she should, but she was wasting precious time.

She pulled into the parking lot at Elkana just as David was getting into his police cruiser.

"David! I need to talk to you," she said, jumping off her bike.

"What's the matter, Jan, what's happened?" he asked, motioning her to get in the police car.

The rain drummed on the roof as Jan quickly related her discovery. She was so excited, the story came out in a one-line rush.

"Put your seat belt on, Jan," David said. "We're going for a little drive." She buckled up as David headed out of the parking lot.

The rain had almost stopped by the time they got to the cairn.

"I think we should walk in from here. If there are tracks, I don't want to ruin them with my tires," David said, pulling to the side of the road.

"Good idea," Jan agreed. "We wouldn't want to destroy evidence. I used the old paved road earlier, but don't count on using it. There's a washout and I don't think you could get your car through."

The sun burst through the clouds just as Jan stepped out of the police car. In the east, a spectacular double rainbow lit the sky. She breathed the soft air, thinking the rain-freshened fragrance the most wonderful smell on earth. Together, she and David walked across the open field to the line shack.

Carefully, they made their way around the deserted cabin to the shed in the back. The ground was soaked and small rivulets of muddy water drained away into the kinnikinnick under the pines.

"Jan, I don't see any evidence of the tire tracks you spoke of. The rain must have erased them. Let's have a look in the shed, without disturbing anything. If we need a search warrant, I don't want any smart defence lawyer getting our boy off on a technicality." He and Jan carefully peered through the poorly closed old door.

Inside the old shed, the gloom was almost complete. However, there was enough light to see that the interior of the shed was empty.

Jan shook her head. "This can't be possible," she said, clenching her fists. "I saw a bike in there less than two hours ago."

"Well, it's not there now." He shook his head, and Jan could see the skepticism in his eyes. "Look, I know how much you want to clear Grey. All I'm saying is maybe there's another explanation for what you saw. Are you sure it wasn't just a tourist's bike stashed to get out of the rain? Maybe some biker and his girlfriend were out for a picnic and decided to call it quits when the rain started."

"No, David! That bike was the same one that rode me off the road. I'm sure of it. I don't know how it disappeared, but it was in that shed and Collin Watson put it there!" She was near tears now. She tried to stop, but this was the final straw. She felt her eyes sting as she blinked, fighting back the flood.

"Jan," David said gently, "there are no tire tracks, no evidence there ever were, and the bike is nowhere to be seen. I can't go to Sergeant Gellar with this. I'm sorry." He put his hand on her shoulder, but Jan shrugged it off.

"Okay, fine, I don't know what's going on here, but I'm sure as hell going to find out." She stomped back to the police car, slamming the door.

David followed, looking, Jan noted with satisfaction as she wiped at her tear-streaked face, as disappointed as she was.

He drove her back to pick up her bike. She was trying not to do two stupid things at once — cry and get angry. Neither one would do Grey any good.

She was just climbing onto her bike when David got out of his car and walked over to her.

"Jan, I know you're upset, but I've got to be honest with you. You're beginning to sound like the boy who cried wolf. I just hope that one day that wolf doesn't end up snapping at your heels."

Kicking her bike over hard, she was glad when it started and the revving of her engine drowned out any further discussion.

# Chapter 10

After leaving David, Jan rode back to town to talk to Josh. She waited beside his shiny new bike, admiring the sleek lines and beautiful detailing. Josh would be done early today and she really needed a friend. She hoped he wasn't busy after work.

She watched the thunderheads receding in the east. Saskatchewan wheat farmers would be saying a fervent prayer that the hailstorm didn't hit them and instead, just kept on going to Manitoba. A few minutes of hail could bankrupt a farmer for the year. Jan said a little prayer for the Manitoba farmers as well. They didn't know what was coming.

Finally, she saw Josh's lanky form leaving the restaurant with Shauna, one of the new waitresses. Her cute blonde ponytail bobbed gaily as they strolled down the boardwalk, Shauna giggling at something Josh had said.

Jan waved, hoping to catch his attention. A slight nod of his head let Jan know he'd seen her. He made one last comment to Shauna, which made her laugh loud enough for Jan to hear it right across the parking lot, then left and headed toward his bike.

"How'd it go with Constable McKenna?" he asked, grinning.

"Not so good," she said despondently. "We drove back up to the cabin, but when we got there, the bike was gone and the rain had erased any trace of there ever being one. No bike, no tire tracks, no evidence." She looked up at Josh and frowned. "This is bad, Josh. David thinks I've been crying wolf, which is like saying I've been making the whole thing up all along."

"Maybe you should ease up. The cops are working on this case; they'll get Collin." He slipped into his new leather jacket. Jan admired the way it fit him like a glove.

"You're saying I should just wait for *Gellar* to turn something up on Collin? Well, I can tell you right now, that's not going to happen," she said, her frustration letting anger bubble to the surface.

Josh zipped his coat up with a quick yank. "Look, Jan, why won't you take some good advice and leave it alone. Keep that trip to Banff in mind; you could get hurt. I really don't want that to happen." He shrugged his shoulders. "You gave it your best shot, but it didn't work."

Jan was stunned. Even if he was thinking of her safety, she didn't understand his attitude. She wasn't one to throw in the towel.

"I'm not going to give up now, Josh. I'm so close. The stakes are too high. We're talking about my brother going to jail for a crime he didn't commit and with Gellar involved, it would be for a long time. Don't you see? I can't quit." Her throat felt tight. This was not what she'd expected from him. She had counted on his backing her 100%, no question. She felt alone and abandoned.

Pulling her helmet on with a jerk, Jan jumped on her bike and left before Josh could say any more.

Her eyes stung all the way home.

When she walked into the kitchen, her mom took one look at her and put the kettle on for tea. She was good at figuring out when to say something and when to do something.

Jan went directly into the living room and flopped onto the couch.

Her mom made the tea, poured Jan a cup, and brought it in to her.

"I made a good strong cup; you look like you could use it. Let me know if you want to talk." She smiled at Jan and went back to the kitchen.

Jan curled up on the couch with her tea. She hugged a pillow to her with her free hand as she watched a busy squirrel eat sunflower seeds out of the window feeder.

The squirrel's little hands were tiny and quick. Jan watched as the little ball of fur made trip after trip to the feeder. It would stuff its cheeks full of food, then scamper back to an old hollow in a poplar tree a little way from the house. This was probably where it had its nest, thought Jan, sipping on her tea.

When a couple of large blue jays tried to take over the feeder, the feisty squirrel chased them away. It never ceased in its primary job of gathering food for its young. It had a purpose and wasn't going to let anything deter it.

Some things were worth the extra effort. You just couldn't let anything get in your way. She smiled at the squirrel and decided to put more food out for it later.

She finished her tea, feeling a lot better. The tension in her neck had almost all gone.

Her mom was going to an evening Mass in Calgary — with David. If it weren't her mom and David, she'd say those two were an item. The idea of her mom on a real date with David was not one Jan had considered, but when she thought about the possibility, she had to smile.

As she continued to sit and think, Jan tried to understand Josh's change in attitude.

And what was with that business about NoKaOi today? Of all the times to get his information wrong ... She sighed, if only she and David had gotten to the line shack a little earlier. She was sure they could have caught Collin red-handed retrieving the bike. Case closed on Mr. Watson!

She started thinking about that bike. What if Collin hadn't fenced it yet? He couldn't leave it out in plain sight. He'd have to take it back and re-stash it at the shack. And even if he did steal a new one, if he thought the shack was still safe, he'd take it back there and hide it.

She knew what she was going to do. She would stake out the line shack herself and wait for him. She was going to see this through to the end. The idea of action made her feel strong with renewed energy.

She had a sudden brainstorm. Running downstairs to Grey's room, she began rummaging in his closet. Then she saw it. Grey's fancy little Olympus camera he'd bought himself as a reward for holding down the same job for one year. Grabbing the camera, she checked to see if the battery was still good. The little red indicator glowed in the dim light of the closet. Great! Now all she needed was some low-light film and she was all set.

She'd stake out the cabin and take a picture of Collin with the stolen bike. If she waited until nightfall, she would be less likely to be seen. She was tough, but definitely no match for two angry crooks. She would be able to conceal herself better if she took the photo evidence under cover of darkness and with Grey's nifty little camera, she should have no problem.

Once she had the goods on dear Mr. Watson, she'd hightail it out of there with no one the wiser. Even Gellar couldn't ignore a picture that said a thousand words.

She'd wait for her mom to leave for Mass, then head out to the Kananaskis and the shack. When it was all over and she had the pictures, she'd tell her mom about the plan. She didn't want her mom to worry, or worse, forbid her from doing it altogether. Being up in the forestry reserve alone, in the dead of night, with cougars, bears and wolves prowling around was not something Jan thought her mom would allow ... or David. No sense crying wolf to him again either. She'd do this alone.

Soon after her mom and David left, she dressed in her black jeans and jacket to make herself less visible, tucked the camera with its special film she'd bought in her pocket and headed out to the line shack.

She knew the road to the shack would be wet and her bike would leave tracks in the fresh mud, so she decided to take the old paved shortcut. When Collin came back, she didn't want him suspecting someone had found his hideout.

She remembered about the washout, which would have been deadly if she hadn't been paying attention. She was so paranoid; she kept her bike in first gear for that entire stretch of road. The pavement was eroding at a fantastic rate. She hoped it wouldn't make the road impassable before she had a chance to get Collin on film with the goods.

Finally, after a wet and sloppy ride, she made it to the deserted cabin. The engine noise of her bike sounded very loud in the hushed evening air. Hiding her bike in a secluded copse of trees a short distance from the shack, she quietly threaded her way through the underbrush and deadfall to a vantage spot where she could see into one of the windows. She felt invisible in her black jeans and coat as she hid in the trees. Now all she had to do was wait for Collin to show up.

The night drew in around her, bringing a veil of darkness that was lit by millions of sparkling points of light.

She looked up at the silent stars, which were flung across the sky like diamonds. It was breathtaking and Jan couldn't help but think of her mom at church, talking to a god who may be responsible for this incredible display.

A sudden rustling of leathery wings made the hair stand up on the back of her neck. Her muscles tensed and she jumped. Chiding herself for being so nervous, she took a deep breath and let it out slowly. It was only a brown bat feasting on the plentiful supply of flying insects that buzzed around Jan's head.

She took another calming breath and went back to watching. By eleven o'clock, she was getting very cold and stiff. Somehow, she didn't think anything was going to happen tonight. She knew she'd have to get back before her mom and David or she'd have a grilling as to where she'd been and why.

She slowly got to her feet, her cramped legs uncooperative, and mentally filed a memo to herself to remember to bring a blanket tomorrow night. The ground was wet and the cold stabbed into her bones like daggers of ice. If Grey were here, he'd call her a sissy. The thought of her brother made the cold more bearable. She was doing this for him.

The trip home was chilly as the damp night air pulled at her numbed legs and arms. She made another note to herself to put an extra sweater on over her sweatshirt for tomorrow night. This sleuthing business required more preparation than she thought.

The house was dark and quiet when she got home. Jan figured her mom and David must have stopped for a bite to eat after church. She was glad for the extra time. Her muscles ached and it took her longer than usual to put her bike away. As quickly as she could, she hurried into the house and up to bed before her mom got home.

* * *

The next day dragged by. Robin came into work early and was the only bright spot in an otherwise routine shift at the restaurant.

It was Josh's day off. Jan was glad. She didn't want to argue about her plans for the evening.

Finally, Jan cashed out and left for home. She decided she'd tell her mom she had a date tonight, and that way there wouldn't be a problem with getting in late. In a way, it was actually true. She had a date — with Collin Watson. She just hoped she wouldn't be stood up again.

* * *

"That's an odd outfit for a date, January. Are you sure you don't want to put on something with a little more colour?" her mom asked when Jan came downstairs dressed all in black.

"Nope, this will be most appropriate, Mom." Jan gave her mom a quick kiss, then headed for the back porch to get her helmet.

"What time will you be home," her mom asked as Jan started out the back door.

"I'm not sure. Don't wait up," Jan called, closing the door behind her.

She hadn't been able to grab a blanket to sit on. She'd forgotten to put one out with her bike until it was too late. Her mom would have given her the third degree if she had taken a blanket on a late-night date.

Her bike started, first kick. She'd have to tell Grey how well the little machine was holding up. Her mom had said he was recovering at a faster rate than the doctors had expected. Jan smiled; she was going to get her brother back again. Her job was to keep him out of jail once he was healed.

She took the shortcut to the line shack again. She was getting used to the washed out pavement and could make better time on the old paved road.

The trees surrounding the cabin sighed in the warm westerly breeze. Jan knew the gentle wind would cease later. Right about the time she started seizing up with the night damp, she thought, as she stashed her bike in a dense bunch of pines by the cabin.

Going back to the previous night's well-hidden spot, she settled in to wait.

As the darkness grew more intense, Jan listened to the familiar sounds of the forest. Everything was exactly as it had been last night. She looked at the luminous dial on her watch. Ten-thirty. She could maybe stretch her *date* out until midnight, but any later than that and her mom would start worrying.

She was thinking about what excuse she would use tomorrow night, when she thought she heard the sound of a motor far off in the distance.

She held her breath and listened. It was definitely a motor and it was getting closer.

Her heart began to pound. This could be it.

She waited, muscles tense as the noise got louder. She could just make out two distinct motor noises — one of a heavy vehicle, like a truck or van, and the other, more rumbly, with a throaty resonance. She was sure the second motor was that of a big bike — like a CBR 900RR Fireblade!

Jan felt her pocket to make sure the camera was there. Through the forest gloom, she saw lights bouncing off the trees. They were coming toward her.

She watched as a large van, followed by a motorbike, pulled into the clearing in front of the cabin. The guy on the bike wore black leathers and a black helmet with a lightning bolt design. He got off the bike and sauntered into the cabin. Jan's adrenaline was pumping double and she was sure either Collin or the big gorilla he was with would be able to hear her heart racing.

The big gorilla was an older man with long, greasy hair pulled back in a ponytail and a scraggly beard cut in a goatee. He wore a torn T-shirt and ratty brown leather vest on the back of which was a picture of a skeleton riding a chopper.

Jan thought that was pretty cliché. Obviously, this guy had no imagination.

She waited until they'd gone inside the darkened cabin, then started inching her way through the trees toward the building. She'd use the van as a screen. She had to cross some open ground in front, but if she was careful, she could keep out of the window's direct line of sight. Taking a deep breath, Jan dashed for the side of the van.

There was no reaction from inside the cabin. She'd made it. Leaning up against the cold metal, she reached inside her jacket pocket and took the small camera out. Her hands were shaking and her fingers were cold. She swallowed and peered around the edge of the van.

A lantern came on inside the cabin and Jan could hear murmuring voices through the open window. It had no glass and the wooden shutters were open to the cool night air.

The open shutters would make taking her pictures easier. The only catch would be to avoid having the camera spotted as she took them. With the special low-light film she'd bought, she shouldn't need a flash, but they might still see the camera as she poked it in through the window. It could get tricky. She edged closer to the front of the van.

She was so scared, her breath came in small gulps. She could see the fence in the window. His back was to her, blocking her view of the inside of the cabin.

142

She knew if she were going to get a picture of Collin with the fence, she'd have to get closer. In fact, she'd have to get directly beside the window, shoot into the cabin, and hope there would be enough light inside for the picture to work. Even fancy film needed some amount of light.

She waited, timing her moment. Then, just as the fence moved out of sight, she dashed to the side of the cabin. She stood absolutely still, listening. Jan could hear him talking about money. She felt along the old logs as she inched toward the window.

She'd almost made it when she heard something she didn't expect. It was the sound of another vehicle approaching. She froze. If another car came into the clearing, she'd be caught in the headlight glare and spotted immediately. The noise got louder. It was a car and now she could see the headlights' glare turning off the road and heading toward the cabin.

She could feel the dark edge of panic plucking at her with sharp, bony fingers. If she'd been hooked up to one of Grey's electronic monitors, she was sure the alarm would be screaming at the rate her heart was pounding.

She couldn't make it to her bike, whoever was driving the car would see her. She crept back along the rough log wall. Her only chance was to try a dash to the old shed behind the cabin. She couldn't be seen from there. Once whoever it was went inside, she could still take the pictures she so desperately needed.

As quietly as possible, she ran from the back of the cabin to the old shed where she'd first seen the bike hidden. Darting behind the ramshackle outbuilding, she waited for the pounding in her ears to stop so she could listen. She heard a car door slam. Then the old screen door to the cabin opened and closed again as someone entered.

Jan listened, but she was too far away to make out who was speaking. Avoiding a puddle she'd nearly run into on the way to the shed, she sprinted to the back wall of the cabin.

Peering around the corner of the logs, she couldn't believe what she was looking at. It was Collin's car! But who'd brought it here?

She started moving along the wall toward the window. It was even more important now to get those pictures. She hadn't expected a third man and she doubted the cops had either.

Jan checked the camera. She had to be sure the flash was disabled. That would be a disaster. She was just about at the edge of the windowsill, when a sudden movement inside the cabin made her freeze.

She held her breath as the guy with the ponytail reached out and pulled both shutters on the broken window closed with a bang.

Her legs went limp.

This was getting quite complicated and she was becoming really scared. Jan debated what to do. She needed help. The camera plan had just become obsolete.

If she could get David McKenna up here, they could capture the whole motorcycle ring at once. There would be no need for pictures, just lawyers. But how?

Then she remembered something that could solve her problem. When she'd searched Collin's car, she'd found a cellular phone in his glove box. If she could get to it, she could call 911 and get them to send David out here. She said a little prayer that the meeting of the local chapter of Bike Thieves Anonymous would stay in session long enough for her plan to work.

Thinking about her odds of pulling this off successfully, Jan said another prayer. This one was for her.

She could hear laughter coming from inside the cabin. The meeting was still in progress. She still had a chance.

She gauged the distance between her and Collin's car, which was parked beside the van. It was adjacent to the open ground she'd have to cross to get back to her bike. This was a stroke of luck for her. She could swipe the phone and take it with her to her bike. Then call the cops from the relative safety of the covering forest.

She counted on Collin to have a really hi-tech phone with lots of wattage. She would need it. The chances of the phone working from here, with all the mountains and hills for interference, was slim at best.

She waited till she was sure the coast was clear, then bolted for the car. Crouching as she ran, she hoped no one decided to pick that moment to reopen the shutters.

She made it to his car and scrambled around to the driver's door. It was farthest from the cabin and afforded her the best chance of not being seen as she tried for the glove box.

Making her muscles do what she wanted was becoming increasingly difficult as fear kept making her chest tight and her legs numb.

She started to reach for the handle, then stopped and listened. Was that a creaking wooden door she heard? No, it was just two branches of an old tree rubbing together in the night breeze. Her heart started beating again. She could still hear muffled voices coming from inside the cabin.

Her fingers closed on the handle and she gave it a gentle tug.

The noise was deafening! It was the loudest car alarm she'd ever heard. Collin must have had one installed when he'd caught her snooping that day at the garage.

In the next instant she heard the cabin door crash open. They were coming!

# Chapter 11

Panic! Total, utter panic! Her first instinct was to hide, but where? Jan took in her surroundings at a glance. There was nowhere to hide. She felt beads of sweat stand out on her forehead. Now she knew how a deer felt when it found itself trapped in the headlights of an oncoming semitrailer.

Her only option was to try and outrun them. She had to get to her bike. If she could just make it to her bike, she'd have a chance of getting out of there. An extremely slim chance, but a chance.

She forgot about trying to retrieve the phone and scrambled toward the woods. She knew they'd spot her as she crossed the open ground, but she had no choice.

The darkness would work in her favour. It would take their eyes a minute to adjust. Also, she knew where she was going — they didn't.

She could hear voices behind her, yelling, then the sound of splintering wood and a burst of vicious cursing. She remembered the front steps were rotten and broken in places. From the language, she guessed they'd forgotten that little detail.

She kept running. Her legs were burning from the sudden exertion; adrenaline made her muscles work harder than she thought they could.

She'd just made it to the cover of the trees, when she heard one of them say he'd take the van and block her escape on the road.

She scrambled through the deadfall, the trees and bushes tearing at her face and arms. Her hair became snagged in a tangle of branches and she bit back a yell of pain.

Relief washed over her as she saw her bike up ahead. It seemed to be waiting for her, ready to speed out of there just as soon as she could kick over the starter. She pulled her helmet on, yanking the chin strap tight. Her hand shook as she turned the key in the ignition.

If this had been a B movie, the bike wouldn't have started, and the monster would have eaten her. Fortunately for her, Jan thought, this wasn't a bad movie, just a bad dream. The bike caught first try.

Gravel spun as she strained to keep the bike upright while it bounced through the underbrush toward the road. She had to beat the van or she'd be cut off.

She caught a flicker of light in her rearview mirrors. It was the high beams of the van and it was picking up speed. She twisted her wrist on the throttle and the little bike leapt forward.

Her front wheel hit the dirt road and grabbed at a driving surface it could understand. In an instant she was heading down the gravel road far ahead of the lumbering van, which hadn't even made it to the turnoff yet.

Suddenly, a blinding flash in her mirrors made her check over her shoulder. It was the sleek form of the CBR eating up the ground between them. Collin was after her. She knew she couldn't outaccelerate the powerful machine in a straight line. However, her little bike was fast and more than that, it was nimble. If she could evade the big bike long enough on the tightly twisting mountain roads, she just might be able to lose him by circling around on the crisscrossing paths and trails that ran throughout this area and make it back to the police station.

She headed west, hoping Collin, who hated green trees and mountain vistas, wasn't used to riding on loose gravel and rutted backcountry roads. He wouldn't be able to use all his machine's horsepower and she just might be able to stay ahead of him.

She didn't want to think about what would happen if he caught her.

The road was torturous and the corners almost impossible to see before she was in them. She was seriously overdriving her headlight and knew one wrong turn and she'd be done.

The big bike behind her was slowly reeling her in. She had to find some way of outdriving him without getting herself in trouble.

The front wheel suddenly shuddered and bucked as she hit a patch of washboard she hadn't seen. She stood up on the pegs, desperately trying to ride it out without losing too much speed. If she screwed up now, the bike would go down. She hadn't had time to put her gloves on, and she noticed her knuckles gleamed white in the moonlight as she gripped the handlebars.

It was like fighting the world's worst rapids in a canoe with no paddle. It took every ounce of her riding skill just to keep the bike upright. Finally, the road cleared and her bike jumped forward. Jan doubted the heavier CBR with its trick suspension would have as much trouble on the rippled road as she'd had.

Collin could outperform her, outhorsepower her and outmuscle her if she were caught. Her only chance was to disable him completely. Suddenly, a desperate plan came to her.

If she could lure him to the shortcut, she could let him think he could catch her by dropping her speed at just the right moment. Then when he accelerated to overtake her, she'd deke around the corner with the washout, being careful to take the inside line herself, and he'd be into a world of trouble before he could react. She knew he'd take the racing line in order to catch her; it was quicker — except that line lead to a washed-out road and a three-metre drop.

She headed for the shortcut.

The trick would be staying out of his grip until she'd had a chance to set up her trap. She wracked her brain trying to remember how to get back to the road that led to the shortcut. At night, it would be easy to miss a turn in the twisty, rutted tracks that served as roads.

Up ahead she saw a lighter patch in the darkness. It was the demarcation where the cutline ran through the densely treed forest. She knew the cutline intersected the road she needed. It was a gamble her bike could make it up the deforested tract, but her options were running out. She turned off the road and hit the wide cleared strip of wild grass and old tree stumps with a hard thump.

Her little bike bumped and hopped as she drove around debris and over rocks. It really wasn't designed for off-roading, but then, neither was she.

She could see the big CBR following as she threaded her way forward through the obstacle course that was the cutline.

Finally, after a bone-jarring eternity, she made it to the junction with the old paved road. She cranked the handlebars hard right and headed back east. She knew this road and made good time.

Unfortunately, because it was a real road, Collin could really scream down it also. She pushed the little bike harder.

Jan could see the series of turns up ahead that signalled the start of the section with the washout. She slowed her bike until the big CBR was directly in her mirrors. Then, seeing he was going to try for her, she started into the corners.

She heard the smooth, throaty rumble of the other bike's motor accelerating. The washout was just out of sight around the next bend. It was on the outside of the corner, at the exit, so once Collin started into it, he'd be committed. He'd hit the washout as he accelerated out of the turn.

She braked hard, turned in to the corner later than she would have to take the fastest way through, and deliberately forced the bike to the inside. Jan was hugging the rock wall so closely she could have reached out with her foot and touched it.

Unfortunately, she'd miscalculated just how eroded the surface had become. Jan could feel her bike begin to wobble unsteadily as her tires just touched the loose asphalt where the inside edge of the washout began. She gave the throttle a twist that propelled her forward with enough speed that she was able to break free of the rubble and climb back onto solid paved road.

Just in time.

There was a sudden whine as the CBR roared into empty space behind her.

Then a splintering crash as it hit the bottom of the washed-out ravine.

Jan pulled on her brakes and slowed her bike. She turned around and shone her headlight back down the road.

The CBR was nowhere to be seen. Collin had driven right into her trap.

She knew she should drive away — now. She could go back to Bragg Creek and get the police. They'd take care of Collin.

Then she thought of how Grey must have felt lying by the side of the road, broken and in pain. She pictured Collin at the bottom of the ravine, perhaps bleeding. She couldn't leave him. She had to make sure he was okay first.

Slowly, slowly she drove forward until her bike was parked near the edge of the washout.

She climbed off her bike and cautiously approached the ravine that used to be where the road came around the corner.

She couldn't hear anything, but the headlight on the CBR was still on. It was twisted at a crazy angle, pointing upward to the dark sky like some bizarre klieg light. The beam of white light illuminated the dust the bike had kicked up when it crashed.

Jan looked for Collin. She couldn't see him, but he could have been thrown from the bike as it clawed its way through the air.

Suddenly, her stomach tightened. She heard it, and then her mind recognized the sound for what it was.

A vehicle engine was labouring up the rutted road, getting louder as it moved closer. She stared into the darkness. Back down the road, coming right toward her, was the unmistakable glare of two headlights.

# Chapter 12

Jan watched with mounting apprehension as the headlights moved steadily closer. One thing was for sure. She wasn't going to wait for the guy with the ponytail and the unknown accomplice to get here and see what she'd done to their partner.

She was going for the police.

January turned to run to her bike ... and collided directly into someone wearing black leathers!

The unknown assailant grabbed her shoulders to stop her flight. Jan froze. Too shocked to move, she stared up into the dark visor of the lightning bolt helmet.

Then she heard it and her whole body went numb.

She stood rigid in his steely grip, listening to the laboured breathing, which came in ragged, raspy gasps.

Transfixed, she stared at the exaggerated movement of his chest as he tried to pull in more oxygen than his damaged lungs could process. The sound was unmistakable — the wheezing, forced breathing of someone having an asthma attack.

"I took your advice, Jan, and didn't stay with the bike when it crashed."

Jan could only watch as the black-gloved hand flipped up the visor on the helmet.

Staring into Josh's strained face, she felt sick, not wanting to believe what his being here meant.

"Jan, I need your help. You've got to help me get away," he said, his voice a strange strangled sound. Taking his inhaler out of his pocket, he took two deep puffs.

She was stunned. "Josh, *you're* the bike thief! Everything that's happened, the near misses, the trip to Banff, it was you? All this time ..." she said, her heart sinking. "All this time, you've been using me."

Josh adamantly shook his head. "Jan, it's not like that." His face became troubled. "Okay, I'll admit in the beginning, it was the perfect way to find out what the cops were up to next. You fed me all the information Collin and I needed to stay one jump ahead of the law." His voice softened. "But the more I was around you, the more my feelings started to change. You were so easy to get close to ..." He took a step toward her. "That's the problem, Jan. You were so easy to get close to. You were so much fun, so nice ..."

She shook her head violently, not wanting to hear his words, not sure what to believe.

Then suddenly, her confusion dissolved, to be replaced with cold, hard anger. She clenched her fists. "You lied to me!" she yelled. "This whole time, and I believed you. Josh, I trusted you." She could feel the anger turn to tears, which made her even more furious. "How could I have been so stupid. No wonder we never went out on a regular date where other people saw us together. You didn't want them to know you were seeing me. I was just your pipeline to the cops."

"Let me explain," he protested. "Like I said, maybe in the beginning, but then I got to know you and things changed. I really care for you, Jan. I know this sounds like another line, but it's true. Please Jan, you've got to help me get out of here." He reached out for her.

"Don't touch me," she said, pushing his hands away. "I don't believe you." She stumbled backward away from him, her eyes blurred with the tears she was trying not to shed.

Jan felt so betrayed. She'd been so naive, so gullible, not to see it. Turning on him, she lashed out, "What about you and Collin? I thought you hated him?" she asked accusingly, trying to make sense out of everything.

"We decided it would be safer if we pretended we didn't like each other, then no one would connect us if something went wrong and one of us was caught. It was all Collin's plan. It sounded so easy. All I had to do was ride the bikes he'd hot-wired to the hideout. He did everything else; I just went along. I needed the money to get away from this place, to finally be free. It was my only chance, Jan. Don't you see? I had no choice." His face looked tired and defeated in the eerie light of the motorbike's headlight.

Jan thought she might have heard truth in his voice. Just for a second, she understood something of what he was saying.

Josh, sensing her confusion, moved toward her again.

"You and I could leave together, tonight. We could get out of her." He glanced at her bike. "That little rocket of yours could take us back to Bragg Creek and we could ..."

"*We* could nothing Josh," Jan cut him off.

In the fraction of a second she'd hesitated, it had all become clear to her. Josh wasn't just a motorcycle thief. He was a seriously twisted guy. Maybe he did care for her, but that didn't matter anymore. Too much had happened. He was trouble.

Suddenly, another sound drew her attention.

Jan could hear the vehicle as it approached, then stop on the other side of the washout. She heard both doors open and slam shut. This was it; she had little hope of getting away now. It was three against one. The two figures silhouetted in the glaring white headlights advanced toward her and Josh.

She knew her only hope of escaping was to get to her bike. She glanced at the dark forms of the two men as they moved closer, then back to Josh.

"Josh, I've got to go — alone. You and your partners are going to go to jail. I'm sorry ..." She turned away from him and started for her bike.

"I can't let you do that, Jan." His voice was an ominous-sounding whisper.

Grabbing her roughly, Josh threw her to the ground. Turning, he started toward her waiting bike and the freedom it could supply.

Jan closed her eyes and whispered the first real prayer she'd said in a long time.

Jumping up and scrambling forward, she grabbed Josh's arm. Pulling with all her strength, she spun him around. Before he could react, she did the only thing she could think of. She punched him directly in the middle of his chest.

What little air Josh had, whooshed out of his lungs. Crumpling, he fell to his knees, clutching his chest.

Jan didn't wait to see what happened next. She ran to her bike and jumped on.

Revving the throttle, she started to turn the little bike around.

As she started to let out the clutch, a man's hand suddenly closed over hers, forcing the lever back in. The engine redlined, screaming, until Jan rolled back on the throttle.

Releasing the accelerator, she started clawing at the restraining hand.

"Jan, it's me!"

At the sound of the familiar voice, she turned, looking up into the worried face of David McKenna.

Her heart seemed to skip several beats in a row. David, here? Taking a deep breath, she nudged the bike into neutral. David was here! Relief flooded through her and her knees went weak as she shut the bike off and pushed down the kickstand.

She looked over David's shoulder and saw Sergeant Gellar helping Josh unsteadily to his feet.

"Are you all right?" David asked, hugging her.

"I'm fine, now." She felt her whole body shaking as she grinned up into his face. "But how did you find me?"

Sergeant Gellar escorted Josh to the police cruiser where Jan could see Collin and the guy with the ponytail already in the back of the car.

"Do you remember the other day when I told you about the boy who cried wolf? Well, the tricky part of that story was in the end. The wolf actually shows up. I talked to the sergeant and we did some checking. Your pizza poker idea had real merit especially after we talked to Collin's dad about the money. It seems Collin told his dad he'd cashed in some stocks to buy his car and other toys, but when we checked, the brokerage house said Collin had sold those years ago." He smiled at Jan. "It was your excellent work that cracked this case wide open."

Jan's face beamed.

David nodded. "I think this is just the medicine Grey needs. You can tell him yourself tomorrow."

Sergeant Gellar walked up to them.

Jan thought he looked angry, maybe betrayed. "They can't wait to rat on each other," he said disgustedly. "Josh was sticking to his story about it all being Collin's idea, that is he was until the big, ugly guy sided with Collin about who really masterminded the whole thing. Then the truth came out." He looked at her almost apologetically. "I'm sorry to have to tell you this, Jan, but it was Josh who tampered with the hydraulic brake lines on the Bimota so your brother would crash. He was the one who convinced Grey to take the bike for a ride. Then he and Collin followed Grey, waiting for the brakes to fail, which they did. They called in the accident on Collin's cell phone, making sure we were aware it was a stolen bike. That's how this all started."

He shook his head, disbelievingly. "One for the books. It was completely against the odds. The Indian kid really didn't do it."

"*Métis*," Jan said firmly, "The *Métis* kid didn't do it." She smiled at David and Sergeant Gellar.

Gellar gave Jan a grudging look of approval, "Not bad police work, for a *girl*." He turned and walked back to the car.

Jan grinned. Maybe Sergeant Gellar would learn something from all this ... and maybe he wouldn't. She turned back to David.

"That still doesn't explain how you found me. It's a big forestry reserve."

David nodded toward the two passengers in the police car. "The big guy with the ponytail was driving the van, Collin was with him. They skidded off the road into the ditch and were trying to get the van out when we arrived. We thought we'd offer them a lift," he said grinning. "After we picked them up, Collin decided to cut his losses and throw his two partners to the wolves ... He told us everything, including how Josh chased you out

157

here. I remembered your saying you'd used the old paved shortcut and figured you might try to take it back to Bragg Creek." He shook his head in admiration as he surveyed the broken CBR at the bottom of the ravine. "I must say, I'm impressed at your ingenuity."

Jan suddenly thought of her mom. "Does mom know about any of tonight's activities?"

"Well, actually, no," David said evasively, knowing Jan's mom would be upset when she found out. "I thought we'd tell her later. I wasn't sure anything was going on until I started doing a little checking. I thought it was odd that you, Josh and Collin were all away from Bragg Creek at the same time. You're right," he said, smiling at her. "I don't believe in coincidence. That's when I talked to the sergeant and we decided to come out here."

He whistled softly. "I'm going to have to do a lot of explaining about this to your mom."

Jan grinned. "I'd say it will probably take you the next twenty-five years to talk your way out of this one, Constable. It's the whole letting one of her kids get into danger instead of making them stay home with milk and cookies thing with her, you know."

David nodded. "Yeah, that's about what I figure it will take too, give or take a few years."

"Give or take a few years," Jan agreed.

"I suppose we better get the Dillinger gang back to the station. Will you be able to ride in on your own?" he asked, looking at Jan's bike.

"Hey, it's a great night for a little ride. I'll meet you back in town and we can tell Mom together. It might help your case." She glanced at him out of the corner of her eye, grinning.

He walked her to her bike. "You think so?" he asked, smiling at her.

She swung her leg over the seat on her bike. "Couldn't hurt to have a friend on your side." Her voice caught a little as she thought of how Josh had lied to her. That betrayal would stay with her for a long time. Sighing, she gave the kick-start a quick pump and smiled as her little bike started first try.

* * *

Her mom had taken all the news pretty well. She understood why Jan had done what she'd done. And she also knew Grey would want to hear it from her himself.

The trip to the hospital was one Jan actually looked forward to. Even if Grey couldn't remember what had happened before, he could remember what was happening now.

Jan, her mom and David walked through the entrance to the hospital and started toward the ICU.

As they passed the chapel, Jan nodded. "You know, Mom, I wouldn't mind going with you next time you go to Mass."

Her mom gave her a surprised look, then nodded. "Sure, honey, I'd like the company," she said casually.

David didn't say anything.

As they continued making their way down the connecting hallways leading to the ICU, Jan noticed David was holding her mom's hand as they walked. Jan liked that.

Susan was practically bubbling as they walked up to the ward desk in ICU.

"You look in a good mood," Jan said, smiling at the happy nurse, "but then I often have that effect on people," she teased the nurse they'd come to know so well.

"You can go in and see Grey right away if you like." She grinned.

Together, Jan, David and her mom walked into Grey's room.

They were all surprised to see Grey sitting up in a wheelchair. He watched them as they entered.

"Have you been looking after that bike of ours, January Fournier?" Grey asked in a strong, clear voice. "I've got a lot of hours invested in that thing, and I don't want you neglecting it."

Jan stood stalk still. "What? Me? Of course I've been looking after my bike," she stammered, caught off guard.

Then Grey grinned at his sister. He looked practically normal as he sat in the chair.

"Mom, is she telling me the truth?" he asked. "And from the looks of it, I'd say you've got some news for me too, David, I mean Constable McKenna," he said, looking at his mom and David, who were still holding hands.

"Does this mean your memory's back and you can remember the accident?" Jan asked.

Grey's face clouded. "Some ... more all the time. It's like remembering a movie you saw a long time ago."

"At this rate, you'll be home before long, young man," her mom said, giving Grey a kiss on the cheek.

"Oh, Mom, not in front of the constable," Grey said, grinning. "So tell me what's new, or old, most of it's new to me anyway," he said, smiling as he sat back in his wheelchair.

Jan looked from her mom to David. "Well ..." she began. Grey sat rapt as Jan related everything that had happened. "So when Collin was at the poker games, he'd figure out which bike they were going to take from the information supplied by his dad's friends, then make sure he had an alibi when Josh actually stole it and stashed it at the cabin. Josh pretended he could barely handle his new big bike to throw off anyone looking for

160

the expert rider it would take to maneuver the big machines that were being taken. Also, he and Collin let on they didn't like each other, so they wouldn't be connected."

She took a deep breath and went on, "Once I put the newspaper articles, the Banff bike, the pizza connection, Collin's inexplicable source of money and his misleading me about the cairn together with the leathers in his car trunk, it all made sense."

Grey looked a little lost as he tried to keep up with his sister's explanation.

"I just didn't put Josh in the picture as a bad guy. I thought he really liked me and wanted to help." She shrugged her shoulders. "His loss," she said a little too casually, then went on, "and if it hadn't been for Constable McKenna," she said brightly, then stopped. "Mom, can we stop calling David Constable McKenna after you two get married?"

Her mom looked at David, and her face went quite pink.

David laughed. "We'll discuss it then," he said, coming to her mom's defence, then added, "but that sounds okay with me."

Jan smiled and went on, "As I was saying, if it hadn't been for Constable McKenna having faith in me even though it looked like I may have made the whole thing up, it might not have turned out so great. But you could tell the police yourself now," she said, grinning at her brother.

"Tell them what?" he asked, frowning.

"About Collin and Josh giving you the stolen Bimota ..." She looked expectantly at Grey.

"Jan, I said some things were coming back, unfortunately, the stolen bike stuff isn't one of them. I can't remember anything that happened that day. The doctors

161

think I may never recover some of those memories because they hadn't forged deep pathways in my brain yet or some mumbo jumbo. Anyway, the bottom line is I still can't help you with my case, so it's a good thing you went ahead without me." He looked at her and smiled a small, half-smile. "Thanks January."

"It wasn't just me, like I said, David," she said, grinning at her mom, "was on our team too."

Grey's dark eyes grew serious. "Thanks, David. I won't forget it."

Jan shook her head. "That's just what you *should* do, Grey. Let the past go; forget it. Tomorrow hasn't happened yet. You have a chance to make new memories, happy ones."

Grey sighed and nodded and Jan knew he understood.

"And maybe I'll make a few happy ones of my own," she giggled, looking around the room at her family. "As soon as Grey fixes my bike." She shrugged her shoulders at her brother's confused look, then went on, "I had a little problem on my way home from Banff. I'll tell you about it later. Let's see, oh yeah, and as soon as I get those new heated handlebar covers and my new leathers and helmet and ..."